THE NIGHT TOURIST

THE NIGHT TOURIST

Katherine Marsh

Hyperion Books for Children
New York

First Edition
1 3 5 7 9 10 8 6 4 2
Printed in the United States of America

Library of Congress Cataloging-in-Publication Data on file.
ISBN-13: 978-1-4231-0689-0
ISBN-10: 1-4231-0689-X

Reinforced binding
Book design by Ellice M. Lee
Visit www.hyperionbooksforchildren.com

To Julian and my parents

THE NIGHT TOURIST

I | The Accident

It was just after dusk when the accident happened. As usual, Jack Perdu was walking through the Yale University campus with his nose buried in Ovid's *Metamorphoses*. Although he was only in the ninth grade, he had an after-school job helping the head of the university's Classics department on her new English translation. It was the day after Christmas so there were no professors around, which meant that there was no reason for Jack to look up out of his book. But suddenly he heard a shout.

"Hey, Jack!"

Jack stopped walking and looked up. A girl in a puffy blue parka was running toward him across the brick walkway between the Yale library and Elm Street. Her hair was in braids, and she was frantically waving at him.

"It's Tanya," she panted when she reached him. "I'm in your English class."

"Oh," said Jack. He knew who she was, but, like most

3

of the kids at Hyde Leadership High School, she'd never spoken to him before.

"I was just going to the store to return this pair of pants my mother got me for Christmas," she explained, pulling a pair of brown corduroys out of a plastic bag. "They're pretty awful, aren't they?"

Jack, who was wearing a pair of pants very much like them, didn't say anything. Tanya didn't seem to notice. "Anyway, I can't remember what book we're supposed to read over break. When I saw you, I knew you'd know."

"*Of Mice and Men*," said Jack.

Tanya grinned. "I bet you've read it already."

Jack gave a noncommittal shrug. He'd actually read it a few years earlier.

"You live here, right?" Tanya pointed vaguely at the stone residential colleges, which surrounded the walkway on either side.

Jack nodded.

"And let me guess, your dad's a professor?"

"He's the chair of the Archeology department."

Tanya smiled. "That's why you're so smart. You know every poem in class before we even read it."

"Not really," he murmured, though he usually did.

"Is your mom a professor too?"

Jack shivered and pulled his cap tighter over his unruly thatch of hair. "No," he said. "She's dead."

"Oh my God, I'm so sorry!" said Tanya.

"It's okay. It happened a long time ago. I was six."

Tanya's eyes widened. "What happened?"

Jack looked around her for an escape route. "A scaffold fell on her in New York City," he murmured. "It was a windy day."

"That's horrible!"

"It happened a long time ago," he repeated. Eight years ago this month, he thought, but didn't say it. He looked down at the book in his hands.

"What are you reading? It doesn't look like the *Mice and Men* book."

Jack held up the book so she could see the spine.

"*Metamorphoses.*" Tanya wrinkled her nose. "Is that a book about insects or something?"

"It's a book of Greek myths."

Tanya shook her head. "You're too smart to be in high school, Jack. You should be a professor or something yourself."

"I've got to go," he said. And before she had a chance to say anything else, he flipped open the *Metamorphoses* and started walking toward Elm Street. He'd heard it all before.

As he hurried away, Jack focused on how to properly translate the Latin word *occidit*. He had just started Book Ten of the *Metamorphoses*, which contained his favorite myth, the story of the musician Orpheus. After a snake-bite kills his bride, Eurydice, Orpheus descends into the underworld to bring her back. Jack had gotten as far as the snake attack, after which Eurydice *occidit. Occidit* could mean that the snake "killed her" or "cut her down," but it could also mean that she "perished." Some people might not think there's much of a difference between these possibilities, but Jack did. You could perish in an accident and no one is to blame. But when you're killed, a killer—in Eurydice's case, the snake—is at fault.

Jack stepped onto the crosswalk, his feet feeling ahead of him as his nose stayed pointed like a weather vane into his book. "To be killed, to perish," he murmured, weighing the possibilities. Just as he registered the grammar and settled on the word "perish," exonerating the snake from any intentional wrongdoing, he heard Tanya shout, "Jack!" But he lifted the book closer to his face, pretending not to hear. The next thing he knew, there was loud, heavy metal music, and he was knocked off his feet and into the air.

Jack barely had time to register what had happened. He caught a glimpse of the car that hit him, heard panicked shouts, and closed his eyes as his body hit the ground. A loud rushing sound filled his ears. Then he blacked out.

When Jack came to, he could hear voices talking over

him, at first high-pitched like insects and then slow and demon-like. A wave of nausea passed over him, and he felt too tired to open his eyes. His ears began to adjust themselves to the voices. "He's a very lucky boy," said one. "He has a few bruises on his chest and legs, but no internal injuries. He should be waking up. . . ."

"Are you sure he's okay?"

Jack's eyelids flickered. This voice was his father's.

"The medics . . . when they found him . . ."

Jack could hear a loud sniffle. Even in his semiconscious state, he wondered if his father was going to cry—the way he did late at night after Jack went to bed. The one time Jack had mentioned it, his father had stiffened and told him that he had been dreaming.

"We'll keep him here overnight for observation just to be sure. But I can assure you, Professor Perdu. We did CAT scans, X-rays . . . a dozen different tests. It was a shock to his system, but he's a strong, healthy boy."

"Thank you," his father said softly.

There was the sliding noise of a curtain being closed as the doctor departed.

With great effort, Jack opened his eyes. He was lying on a cot surrounded by a white curtain. He looked at his father, who was blinking back tears.

"Dad?"

His father gripped Jack's hand in his own, something

he hadn't done in years. He had a full, gray beard, and was much older than the fathers of Jack's classmates. He cleared his throat. "How do you feel?"

Jack carefully stretched his arms and legs. Nothing hurt, but he felt stiff, like he'd just run a marathon. He propped himself up on his elbows. "Not too bad for being hit by a car."

His father chuckled. The tears in his eyes, Jack noticed, had dried. "Tough kid," he said, letting go of his hand. "You scared that girl, though, half to death." Jack suddenly remembered Tanya and lay back on the cot. He imagined her telling the other kids at school about the accident. He pictured them laughing as Tanya explained, "I was shouting at him, but he wouldn't even look up from his book."

His father leaned over him. "Are you okay?"

Jack nodded, unable to explain.

His father frowned. "What's your last name?"

"Perdu."

His father looked unimpressed.

"Perdu," Jack repeated, propping himself back up on his elbows. "It means 'lost' in French, from the Latin *perdo*. To destroy, to do away with, to lose."

His father nodded. "How old are you?"

"Fourteen. I'm fine, Dad, really."

His father continued to stare at him. "What's your mother's name?"

Jack paused. His father hardly ever talked about his mother. And Jack never mentioned her, even though he had hundreds of questions. He wished there were someone he could ask about her, but there was no one else in New Haven who had known her. Neither of his parents had siblings, and his grandparents had died long ago.

"Anastasia," Jack answered.

He waited, but his father just nodded and then looked away. "Get some rest," he said. "We'll take you home tomorrow."

Jack tried to stay awake in case his father wanted to talk more, but his silence—punctuated by the beeps and pages of the hospital—seemed only to grow louder and more resolute. Finally, Jack gave up, and closed his eyes.

At first, when he woke up, he didn't know if it was day or night. The fluorescent light of the hospital hallway was inconclusive. His father was lolled in a chair by his bed, snoring. The white face of the clock in his room read four a.m. A nurse in a white uniform stopped in front of the door to his room to greet an emaciated old man in a hospital gown. Jack closed his eyes and tried to fall back asleep, but he couldn't help following their conversation.

"My brother died in New York," said the old man.

Jack thought he heard the nurse say, "We should all be so lucky." But that seemed like an odd thing to say.

"Oh, things aren't perfect there, either," said the man. "The fountains were down the other week. And there's concern that someone who"—the man whispered something Jack couldn't hear—"could find a way—"

"Down to the ninth floor?" interrupted the nurse. "You know that can't happen."

"But some people say . . ."

"That's just an urban myth. Are you getting out tonight?"

"You bet!" said the patient. "I was thinking of flying around the city."

"Maybe I'll join you. Nobody's dying here," said the nurse with a laugh.

Jack smiled with relief as he realized that the conversation didn't make any sense because he was dreaming.

II | Viele's Map

The next morning, Jack came home from the hospital. He and his dad lived together like two bachelors in a corner apartment in Saybrook, one of the gothic stone residential colleges at Yale. The apartment was filled with books, primitive paintings, and lesser archeological finds. There were piles of ancient Greek drachmas, squat stone vases, shards of bone, plant fossils, broken spearheads, naked face-less figurines, and staring masks that had once been used in religious rites. His father also collected modern trinkets from the places he had gone on digs—Turkish tea sets, hookahs, wooden eggs, African flutes, even a voodoo doll that made Jack shiver whenever he walked by it.

Jack was a little sore, but otherwise he felt fine. Still, his father hovered over him, insisting that he stay in bed. Jack didn't mind—he liked his room, which had a window looking out over the stone courtyard below. His floor was littered with dirty clothes and crumpled-up attempts at translations. His walls were covered with maps of countries that no longer existed: the Soviet Union, the Ottoman Empire, Austria-Hungary. He had started the collection with a map of Zanzibar after his mother died. On his dresser sat a silver frame with a photo of her—a pale, dark-haired woman standing on a New York City street corner. The photo was slightly overexposed, but Jack liked his mother's intense gaze and the way her eyes seemed to follow him around the room.

He spent the rest of the morning working on the first section of Book Ten. Just after one, his father knocked on the door with a special treat—a greasy bag of cheeseburgers from the Yankee Doodle grill. After eating three of them, Jack translated a few more lines of the *Metamorphoses* before he yawned and closed the book. Minutes later, he was asleep.

When he woke up from his nap, it was dark. An icy rain pelted the window. The room felt airless, like the inside of a submarine. He stood up, bleary-eyed, and opened the window. Cold air rushed in. The stone courtyard looked slick and shimmery. Grabbing a sweater, he padded his way into the living room. "Dad?" he called out.

No one answered. He wondered if his father had gone out. Jack walked past the piles of drachmas and fossils and looked out the window into the opposite wing of the college. Usually he could see students moving across their rooms or the blue glow of their computer screens. But everyone was away, and there wasn't a single light on. The only face he saw, reflected in the window, was his own.

The door to his father's study slammed shut, and Jack jumped. "Dad?"

Again there was no answer. Jack tiptoed past the voodoo doll and toward his father's study. Through the door, he could hear the steady crackle of opera music from the classical station his father always played. As the chorus picked up, Jack took a deep breath and slowly turned the doorknob. He opened the door a few inches and peered into the study. The first thing he noticed was that the window had blown open and pellets of ice were landing on his father's desk. The same gust of wind that had blown the window open had probably slammed the door shut as well. Jack grinned. It was nothing but a storm.

He began to walk across the study toward the window. But three steps in, he froze. Reclining on the leather couch, his shoes propped up on the armrest, was a lanky man with gray, disheveled hair. Jack stared at the stranger, but the man took no notice of him. He studied a piece of paper, tracing something on it with his finger.

As Jack took a step backward in alarm, the wood floor creaked under him. The man looked up at Jack, then back down to the piece of paper in his hands. "Oh, the window," he murmured, shaking his head, "I guess I shouldn't have opened it. Silly me."

"Who are you?" Jack asked.

With a loud shout, the man leaped off the couch and dropped the piece of paper. His eyes bulged at Jack. For a moment, they just stared at each other. Then the stranger ran to the open window and, without a word, jumped out of it.

Jack dashed to the window and looked out at the courtyard. There was no sign of a body. The courtyard was empty.

He slowly closed the window, leaning on the sill for support. His legs felt weak, and his pulse throbbed in his temples. He thought that he might be dreaming again, but when he poked the bruise on his leg, it definitely hurt. As he stared at the mess of papers on his father's desk, he realized that the top drawer—which was always locked—was open. As he touched the handle, a shiver shot up his arm. The wood felt as cold as a handful of snow. He banged it shut and jerked his hand away.

There was a crash from the other room and the sound of heavy footsteps marching across the apartment. Jack imagined the man who had jumped out of the window returning, his head bashed in from the cobblestones, his hands reaching for him. He scanned the study, frantically looking for a place to hide. But there was no time; the footsteps were right outside the door. He swung around, his fists raised. "Go away!" he shouted.

The door swung open.

"Jack!" his father said. "What's wrong?"

Jack lowered his fists and took a deep breath. "Dad," he said, his voice shaking.

"Of course it's me. Who else would it be?" his father asked. "I just went out to get some dinner. What's wrong? Are you okay?" He gave Jack a strange look.

Jack slipped away from him and sat down on the couch. "I'm fine," he said. "It's just . . ." *It's just a strange man was sitting on the couch and then he jumped out the window. . . .* No, he couldn't say it. His father might take him back to the hospital, this time to the psychiatric ward.

"Just what?"

Jack shook his head.

"It's okay," said his father. "I'll make you some tea."

Jack nodded and his father left the room. There was only one rational explanation for what had happened. His brain had been damaged by the accident. The man and the open desk drawer were hallucinations.

But then Jack's eyes fell on the piece of paper that the stranger had dropped, which was still lying on the floor. Jack wondered if the man had taken it from his father's desk. He tiptoed over and gave it a poke. It didn't vanish or jump out the window. He picked it up.

It was a faded map of Manhattan, unlike any Jack had ever seen. Sections of the island were colored dark green, others light green, and still others, orange. There was a street grid. Green squiggly lines traversed the grid like subway tracks. In the upper left-hand corner, in ornate old-fashioned lettering, was printed: *Sanitary & Topographical Map of the City and Island of New York. Prepared for the Council of Hygiene and Public Health of the Citizens Association Under the Direction of Topographical Engineer Egbert L. Viele.* In tiny printed letters in the lower left-hand corner was a date—1865. Underneath the date, in his father's scratchy handwriting, was the name "Anastasia."

III | Dr. Lyons

Sitting on his bed in his pajamas, Jack anxiously pried open the frame that held his mother's photo. The night before he had stashed the map inscribed with her name there. But in the morning light, he suddenly doubted that the map had been real. He was sure the whole night—the ice storm, the stranger, his leap out the window, the piece of paper he'd left behind, even the sounds of his father crying just before he fell asleep—had been a dream. But when he pulled open the velvety back of the frame, he found the map still lodged inside.

A knock sounded on his door. "Jack? Are you up?"

Jack quickly put the frame back together. His father opened the door and watched him fiddle with the metal tabs. "I'm just straightening Mom's photo," Jack said.

From the way his father was glumly staring at the photo, Jack was pretty sure that he hadn't seen the map. There was an embarrassed silence between them. "How did you sleep?" his father asked.

Jack shrugged. "All right."

"You seemed jumpy last night." His father sat down on the bed and studied the maps on his wall. "After you went to bed I called Dr. Lyons."

Jack put down the photo. "Doctor who?" He'd never heard of a Dr. Lyons before.

"He's an old friend, a doctor in New York. He wants to take a look at you."

Jack thought of the strange man jumping out of the window and frowned. "Does he think there's something wrong with me?"

His father waved a hand dismissively. "No. But I want him to see you, to give a second opinion. So I'm sending you to New York."

Jack was worried. Perhaps Dr. Lyons really did think there was something wrong with him. But then a larger realization dawned on him: he was finally visiting New York. He'd always wanted to go there, but his father had always found some excuse not to take him. It was the place where his mother had died. "Are you coming too?" he asked.

His father shifted uncomfortably. "You need to go yourself. We'll just put you on the train to Grand Central and you'll take a cab to Dr. Lyons's office. When you're done, you'll take the train back home. You'll be fine."

"It doesn't sound like a big deal," said Jack, although

he very much felt the opposite. He had flown alone to Greece to meet his father on a dig the previous summer, but there was something special about going to New York, his mother's city, by himself. He tried to think of a way to say this to his father, but instead he just ended up staring at his mother's photo. His last memory of New York was one of her. He remembered standing in front of a snow-covered fountain, holding the cord to his sled in one mittened hand and her hand in the other. They had sledded in the park all afternoon, and his cheeks stung. But when he tugged his mother's arm to go home, she didn't move. "Come on, Mom," he said. But she didn't seem to hear him, and when Jack looked around, he realized it was getting dark and that they were alone. "Mom!" he shouted. She immediately crouched down and smiled at him. "What?" He knew then that it was okay.

But after she died, it was the moment when she wouldn't answer him that he thought about most.

After lunch, Jack and his father took a taxi to Union Station. As they stood on the platform waiting for the train, Jack opened up the *Metamorphoses* and reread the passage about the *auspicium*, or omen, that foreshadows Eurydice's snakebite. During the wedding ceremony, a torch carried by Hymen, the god of marriage, begins to sputter and smoke. This was considered a bad omen, an *auspicium gravius*, but all omens weren't necessarily bad. In fact, Jack reminded himself, *auspicium* was the root of the English word "auspicious."

As the train chugged toward them, his father handed Jack his cell phone, Dr. Lyons's address, and four twenties. "Call to let me know what train you're coming back on," he said. "And be careful."

There was something about the way his father's face softened that made Jack suddenly think he could ask him about his mom. Not something big, like why his father never talked about her, but something small, like whether she had liked living in New York or what had made her laugh or whether she had any irrational fears. But as swiftly as the softness had come over it, his father's face reassembled into its usual stern expression. After an awkward, silent hug, Jack boarded the train.

Five minutes later Jack was on his way to New York. He took out the Viele map and began charting his route from the train station to Dr. Lyons's office. But it was hard to trace it on the map. The street numbers were small and he couldn't decipher the mazy blue lines that branched and looped through Manhattan. He leaned his head up against his backpack and looked out the window at backyards filled with old car parts and washing machines, empty parking lots, the occasional patch of field, yellow and crackled with frost. The sun wafted in and out behind the clouds, illuminating the ice-covered branches of the trees. Birds swooped overhead, landing on the electric wires, fluttering off. Jack's head bobbed.

"Final stop, Grand Central Terminal!"

Jack opened his eyes. His head throbbed and his mouth was dry and metallic-tasting. The train began to plunge into an underground tunnel. As the daylight faded into shadow, Jack's ears began to pop. The lights in the train flickered on and off, illuminating flashes of tunnel covered with red-lettered warning signs and graffiti scrawls.

"Grand Central Terminal! Please check for your belongings before you leave the train. Thank you for riding Metro-North." The train inched wearily to a stop. Jack folded the map and slid it into his backpack. Hoisting the backpack onto his shoulders, he stumbled onto the platform and began to follow the rushing tide of people into the station. The crowd climbed a flight of marble stairs and carryied him up a ramp and out a door. A few minutes later he was in the backseat of a cab, heading downtown to Dr. Lyons's office.

The office, which shared the twenty-third floor with a cleaning service and a piano tuner, was much smaller than Jack expected. The waiting room was empty save for a receptionist with a blue-tinted bouffant, scribbling in a log beside an enormous stack of yellowed papers. As Jack approached, he could make out the letters atop one of the pieces of paper—CERTIFICATE OF DEATH. It seemed as if most of Dr. Lyons's patients hadn't fared well at all. But before he had a chance to turn back, the receptionist looked up.

"You must be Jack," she said. She stood up and gestured for him to follow her down a dimly lit hallway and into an office. "Have a seat," she said, pointing to a worn couch. "Dr. Lyons will be with you in a minute." As soon as he sat down, the receptionist left, closing the door behind her.

The office wasn't much of an improvement over the waiting room. The walls were lined with rows of antique, leather-bound books, their spines sagging and titles peeling. A framed certificate to Augustus Lyons for Distinguished Alumni Service from the George Chapman School hung lopsided on a hook. The most interesting object in the room was a bookcase made out of shellacked tree limbs. It had five glass shelves; on the middle one, Jack noticed a collection of what looked like ancient coins. They were all the same dull, bronze color except for one, which flashed gold. Jack walked over to the shelf and picked it up. The shape of a "Y" was cut out of its center, and around the edges it said GOOD FOR ONE FARE.

Just then, the door opened, and Jack instinctively

closed his fist around the coin. An obese man his father's age, with drooping, caterpillar-size eyebrows, waddled in. "You must be Louis's son," he said in a cheerful baritone. "I'm Dr. Lyons."

Jack felt his face turn red. "I'm just looking."

"As you should. Fascinating stuff, isn't it?" Dr. Lyons joined Jack by the bookcase. "I collect artifacts from the city's past—playbills, baseball cards, restaurant menus, World's Fair memorabilia, subway tokens."

Jack stood stiffly in front of the shelf, fingering the subway token nestled in his palm. He watched Dr. Lyons's face, hoping he wouldn't notice the token's absence. To Jack's relief, after a quick glance at his collection, the doctor pointed to the couch. "Why don't you take a seat?"

Jack sat down and waited for Dr. Lyons to examine him, but the doctor just eased himself into his chair and spent a few awkward seconds doing nothing except staring at Jack. Finally he said, "I heard about your accident. You're lucky to be alive. How do you feel?"

"Fine," Jack chirped. He suddenly wondered whether his father's old friend was a quack. "Are you a medical doctor?" he asked.

Dr. Lyons laughed. "Something like that. So, nothing . . . unusual?"

Jack wondered if he should tell Dr. Lyons about the

man who had leaped out the window, but then he remembered the enormous pile of death certificates and decided against it. Who knew what kind of bad medicine the doctor was practicing?

"You favor your mother," Dr. Lyons declared.

Jack leaned forward. "You knew my mother?"

The doctor laughed. "You look exactly like her."

Jack swallowed. "My dad never talks about her. What was she—?"

"You're a fine, healthy boy," Dr. Lyons interrupted. He opened a drawer and rooted around in it. *"Puer fortunae bonae."*

A boy of good fortune. Jack smiled at the Latin words.

"I hear you're a Classics scholar," the doctor remarked. "Good at dead languages."

"I'm all right, I guess."

Dr. Lyons finally stopped staring at him and pulled out a bulky, ancient-looking camera. "Would you mind if I took your picture?"

Jack shrugged.

"It's a 1947 Polaroid," Dr. Lyons said, as if that explained everything. "First year they made them."

Jack gave an awkward smile as the flash momentarily blinded him.

The doctor waved the photo in the air and then, after a quick glance, slipped it into the left drawer of his desk.

"Sun sets early this time of year. We'd better get you on your way."

Jack knew he was supposed to stand up, but he didn't. "That's it? Don't you want to examine me?"

Doctor Lyons stood and opened his door. "That's not necessary. I think we're all squared away here."

Jack wanted to protest—nothing seemed to be squared away at all. He was also still holding Dr. Lyons's subway token. But there was no easy way now to explain why he had it and give it back. Jack reluctantly stood and walked out. Dr. Lyons closed the office door behind him.

IV | The Whispering Gallery

Jack stood in the main hall of Grand Central Terminal, peering up at the large black boards that listed the trains' timetables. According to the New Haven line departures, he had a half hour till the next train. It wasn't enough time to leave the station, but it also seemed wrong to come all the way to New York and see nothing except Dr. Lyons's ratty office and the inside of a cab. He scanned the hall, decorated with giant wreaths for the holidays, and noticed a small crowd gathered by the information booth, looking up at the cathedral-high ceiling, which was painted a robin's-egg blue and decorated with stars. He slipped over to join them.

"The ceiling is an actual re-creation of the winter sky," explained a gray-haired woman standing in front of the group of tourists. "But the constellations are in reverse, so that you're seeing the heavens from a God's-eye view."

Jack studied the constellations and realized that the Dipper was indeed backward.

"Now I'm going to show you one of Grand Central's many secrets. The terminal was built in 1913 and has two levels. Please follow me this way to the lower one." The tour guide walked across the great hall and turned under an arch. Jack trailed after the group. They descended a ramp beneath large pineapple-shaped chandeliers until they reached a mezzanine. It had an arched tile roof and four marble columns. On one side was a set of glass doors leading to a tiled restaurant called The Oyster Bar. On the other side was a ramp leading to the lower level of the station. The guide pointed to the marble columns. "This is the whispering gallery," she explained. "If you whisper into a column, those standing at the other columns will hear you. Try it. Press your ears against it."

The tourists fanned out, eager to have a turn. Jack walked over to one of the columns. An older woman, leaning her ear into it, turned around to face him. "Do you want to give it a try?" she asked. Jack nodded and put his ear up against the column. He could hear several voices whispering. "Hey, Sarah! Sarah!" "Brian, can you hear me?" "Yoo-hoo, Christopher." It sounded as if they were standing right next to him.

Behind him, he heard the tour guide clap her hands. "Let's move on, now. The sun is about to set, so we're too late to see the pinhole suns on the main concourse; but the compass rose in the subway station will help you find your way home."

Jack lingered in front of the column. He still hadn't whispered anything into it himself, but he couldn't figure out what to say. "Hello," he said in an uncertain voice. He stepped back and looked around, feeling self-conscious. The tourists were leaving the other columns and catching up to the guide. "I liked the stars best of all," said a plump woman to a boy Jack's age as they passed. Jack thought about how he liked the stars too—the whispering gallery wasn't much fun if you had no one to talk to. He suddenly remembered a poem that his father used to read to him after his mother had died. It was by John Donne, the seventeenth-century English poet. Jack leaned against the column and whispered:

"Go and catch a falling star,
Get with child a mandrake root,
Tell me where all past years are,
Or who cleft the Devil's foot;
Teach me to hear mermaids singing,
Or to keep off envy's stinging,
And find
What wind
Serves to advance an honest mind."

Jack paused, trying to remember the next stanza. But

before he could continue, he heard a high-pitched voice coming through the column.

"If thou be'st born to strange sights,
Things invisible to see,
Ride ten thousand days and nights,
Till Age snow white hairs on thee. . . ."

Jack took a surprised step back from the column. The voice was a girl's, one he didn't recognize. He turned around to look for her. But as he scanned the other corners, his stomach tightened. The tour guide had left, and all the tourists were gone. Commuters were rushing through the mezzanine, but no one was standing near any of the columns.

Maybe the girl had spoken into a column and then rushed away to join the tour. But if she was gone, the whispering gallery should now be silent. Jack put his ear back to the column.

"'Thou, when thou return'st, wilt tell me/All strange wonders that befell thee,'" sang the girl's voice.

"Hello?" Jack interrupted.

V | Euri

"'Hello' is not in the poem," said the voice. "I studied it in school. The next line is, 'And swear/No where/Lives a woman true and . . .'"

"Where are you?" Jack asked.

"What do you mean where am I? I'm standing right across from you."

Jack whirled around. Standing in front of a column across the mezzanine was a skinny girl about his own age. Her dirty-blond hair was pulled back in a messy ponytail. She wore kneesocks, a short, pleated skirt, a white blouse, and a navy blue blazer with a yellow insignia. She had a small mouth, which gave her a hard look, and her eyes were a pale, almost translucent blue.

Jack leaned against the column as she walked over to him. "Were you there the whole time you were talking to me?" he asked.

The girl gave him a funny look. "I'm Euri," she said.

"Jack," he murmured.

"Enchantée!"

Jack raised his eyebrows.

"That's 'nice to meet you' in French," she explained. "How old are you?"

"Fourteen."

"Me too!" Euri exclaimed. She continued to stare at him. He smiled nervously. "You're not from around here, are you?" she finally asked.

Jack felt challenged. "Actually, I was born here. But after my mother died—"

"Your mother died here?" Euri interrupted.

Jack instantly regretted mentioning it. "Yeah . . ." he added quickly, "and so after she died, my dad and I moved to New Haven."

Euri had a look of horror on her face. "New Haven?" she repeated. "That's awful!"

Jack didn't know what to say. He'd never met anyone who thought that living in New Haven was worse than having a dead mother. "It's actually much nicer than people think," he stammered.

Euri waved away the rest of his defense as if she'd heard it before. "Are you here by yourself?"

Jack nodded. "I have to go back home soon," he said. "My dad is wait—"

"You want to do some sightseeing?" Euri interrupted again. "I can give you a tour!"

"That's okay." He looked down at his watch to suggest that he had to leave.

"Oh, come on. I know this station inside out," she bragged. "I can show you some really cool places you won't see on the official tour. Only real urban explorers know about them. Like FDR's secret door."

Jack forgot himself and looked her in the eye. "What's that?"

Euri smiled in a self-congratulatory way. "Years and years ago, when President Roosevelt came into town, his train used to stop on a special track in Grand Central. His limo would drive off the train and through this secret door into an elevator. Then he'd go up to the garage of the Waldorf-Astoria hotel and pop out onto Forty-ninth Street without anyone knowing. Pretty neat, huh? Not many people know about it."

Jack looked uncertainly around the whispering gallery. "Is it far from here?"

"Not so far," said Euri. "It's on track sixty-one."

Jack had no idea where track 61 was. He gnawed on his lip. It would be nice to actually see something in New York, especially something that most people didn't know about. He liked the idea of being an urban explorer. His father would understand a short side trip to see something historical, like FDR's secret door. And Euri didn't seem like the type of person he had to watch out for in New

York. She was just a girl his own age, the first one he'd met who didn't seem to feel sorry for him.

Jack looked at his schedule. There was another train to New Haven in forty minutes. He would call his father after he was done exploring to tell him he'd be on that train. "Okay," he told Euri. "I have a half hour, I guess."

VI | Track 61

Jack followed Euri up the ramp into the main hall of the terminal. She was a fast walker, and he had to nearly run to keep up with her. He studied her back and tried to figure out what to say. The uniform caught his eye. It suddenly struck him as strange that she was wearing it during the Christmas holiday. But just as he was about to ask, she glanced back at him. "Not much farther," she said.

Jack studied the main hall of the terminal, but the signs only confused him: all the tracks were numbered up to the low forties, and on the lower level they started in the hundreds. There didn't seem to be any tracks in the sixties. "Are you sure there's a track sixty-one?" he asked.

"Of course there is," she said without even turning around. "But it wouldn't be a secret if it were obvious."

Jack followed Euri onto the platform of track 42. A train was idling alongside it as passengers boarded. He wondered if they were going to get on the train, too, but Euri continued down the edge of the track, past the conductor standing near the door of the last car. Up ahead, in the middle of the platform, Jack saw a brightly lit tile stairway leading down to the lower level. A sign in red letters above it read EXIT.

"Is that where we're going?" he asked.

For the first time since they left the whispering gallery, Euri stopped walking. "Nope. We're going down there."

Jack followed her finger, which was pointing over the end of the platform and onto the tracks.

He backed away. "Is that safe?"

"We're just going down there for a second so we can crawl onto that walkway. Do you see it?" Euri pointed into the darkness. Jack squinted and, sure enough, saw a narrow walkway perched a few feet above the tracks. "Come on," said Euri. "This'll be fun."

She climbed down a small metal ladder that led down to the track, and Jack slowly followed her. Toxic-looking yellow puddles dotted the track. Jack picked his way around them, following Euri till they reached another ladder up to the walkway. Euri turned to him and smiled. "See, that wasn't so bad. It's not far now."

Jack tried to smile back. The air inside the tunnel smelled sharp and electric. As he scurried along the walkway after Euri, he could see rats darting across the tracks below. There were no other people, though he occasionally heard voices and the clanking sounds of machines echoing under the low ceiling of the tunnel. STAY ALERT advised a rusted metal sign bolted to the tunnel wall. Jack paused, wishing he knew exactly where track 61 was and how far Euri was taking him. He stopped to pull the Viele map out of his backpack and squinted at it in the dim light. Tracing the veiny lines with his finger, he realized that they formed a circle around the terminal. But the rest didn't make a bit of sense to him. Euri's pale ponytail bobbed up ahead in the darkness. He stuffed the map back into his backpack and hurried after her.

Suddenly the track below him glinted silver blue. He spun around. A train was rumbling along it toward them.

The locomotive seemed enormous, big enough to squash him against the wall. As it veered around a curve, two white lights bored into him from above. The train honked its horn, as loud as a steamship, and Jack instinctively flattened himself against the wall and shut his eyes. The earth shook, a roar filled his ears, and a blast of hot, burned-smelling air forced him to hold his breath. He wished he had never followed Euri. Scrunching up his eyes, he waited for the locomotive to crush his body. I'm a fool, he thought, and now I'm going to die.

But a few seconds later, the rumbling stopped and a rush of cool air washed over him. Jack opened his mouth and eyes at the same time, gasping as he watched the red brake lights of the train snake away. His legs were quaking and rubbery. He unstuck himself from the wall and looked for Euri. To his surprise, she wasn't pressed against the wall but perched on the walkway railing in front of him grinning. "What are you doing there?" he shouted. "We almost died!"

He expected her to comfort him, but instead she clapped her hand over her mouth and hunched over, stifling laughter.

"What? We nearly did!"

She straightened back up and wiped a tear from her cheek. "I'm sorry. I didn't mean . . ."

But then she dissolved again into silent peals of laughter.

"I should go back now," Jack muttered.

Euri immediately stopped laughing. "Please, don't go. I'm really sorry, it's just . . ." She grinned and shook her head. "We're almost there." Jumping off the railing, she continued down the walkway, coughing softly to disguise a few last giggles.

But Jack didn't follow her. Instead, he looked around the tunnel. A cobweb hung down from the cement ceiling, swinging gently in time with the drafts of air. Jack brushed his hand through his hair. Euri stopped and turned around. "What's wrong? Are you getting freaked out?"

"No," said Jack defensively. "This doesn't scare me."

"What scares you, then?"

The direct way that Euri had of asking questions made it hard for Jack not to answer. "Dogs," he said, surprised by his own honesty. "I was bitten by one once when I was seven."

"I don't like dogs either," mused Euri. "But there aren't any here. Come on."

At this point, he had no choice but to follow her. A light was out up ahead, and he could hear an eerie whistling sound. Euri disappeared into the darkness. "Come on, it's right here," she called. He slowly tiptoed forward, his heart pumping, his legs tingling with adrenaline.

He was on the edge of the darkness. Another step and he was inside of it. A strange warm wind blew through his hair. As his eyes adjusted to the dark, Jack noticed that the walkway ended in a narrow descending staircase, illuminated by a single naked bulb. To his right was a brick wall and a large iron door padlocked shut by a rusty bar.

"Ta-*dum*, track sixty-one!" said Euri, gesturing toward the padlocked door.

But Jack wasn't looking at the door. "Where does that go?" he asked, pointing to the staircase.

"Oh, that leads to the other levels of the station," Euri said. "Want to see?"

Jack took a few steps toward the staircase and looked down. "But the guide said there were only two levels."

"That was the official tour. I'm giving you the unofficial tour. There are nine."

Jack suddenly remembered the dream he'd had at the hospital, how the nurse had mentioned a ninth floor under New York. "Nine?" He looked at Euri, but she crossed her arms over her chest and stared straight back at him.

"Come on," she said, "I'll show you." With a smirk she added, "It's a different world down there."

Jack pinched his arm with his fingernails to make sure he wasn't dreaming. He stared at the red crescents left behind. He thought about his accident. "Let's go," Euri said brightly as she skipped down the stairs. Jack clutched the black cast-iron banister and followed.

VII | Down

"There's something strange about you," Jack called out to the swinging pale ponytail ahead of him. He was surprised by his own boldness. He would never have said this to any of the girls at school. Perhaps that was what was so strange about Euri—that he felt comfortable around her.

"Like what?" Euri replied.

Jack hesitated. They had just passed a cinder block vestibule that marked their second flight of stairs. His hair fluttered gently in the warm wind, and he wondered whether it was the hot air of a furnace below. The bulbs on the ceiling above him flickered.

"Why are you wearing your uniform now? Aren't you on Christmas break?"

The stairway grew suddenly silent so that the only footsteps Jack could hear were his own. He bit his lip. "Euri?"

"I don't want to talk about the uniform," she finally said.

Jack felt his face grow warm.

"Don't feel bad," Euri said, a few moments later. "I just don't want to talk about it, okay? I didn't like the school."

"Okay," said Jack, glad she wasn't angry. Still, her answer didn't seem to make sense.

"So," said Euri. "Why did you come to New York, anyway?"

"I had a doctor's appointment," said Jack.

"Is there something wrong with you?"

"No," he said. "I mean, I don't think there is."

"So the doctor said you were healthy?"

"Yes, why? Do I look sick or something?"

Euri laughed. "No."

Something warm and wet suddenly dropped onto Jack's forehead, and he cried out.

"What is it?" Euri asked.

Looking up, he noticed the cement had dripped into long cones like the stalactites in a cave, and large, shining drops of water hung pendulously from the ends of them. "Nothing," said Jack, his face warm again. "Just water."

By the third flight, the water was dripping at regular intervals and his hair felt damp. Except for the pitter-patter of drops and the gentle gusts of warm wind, there was no sound at all besides their footsteps.

Four. Five. Jack's knees began to ache. On the sixth

level, the bulb was out. By the seventh flight, Jack felt like he'd passed into a dream. The constant ache of his legs stopped. Euri had disappeared around the bend of the next flight of stairs. Jack rounded the corner of the eighth flight and nearly crashed into a stone wall.

There were no more stairs. He had reached the ninth level. But where was he? He could barely see in the dim light. Close by, he could hear water lapping and voices talking over each other in a strange, disembodied way. "Can you hear me?" "Hello, Michael!" "Want to hear a secret?" It sounded as if there were dozens of people standing just around the corner.

"Come on, Jack," Euri called in a voice louder than the rest.

Jack tiptoed forward along the wall until he could see her standing a few feet in front of him in an empty, high-ceilinged room that reminded him of an Egyptian tomb. Thick, stone pillars stretched toward the ceiling, and what looked like a slender canal of murky water flowed through the center of it. Next to the canal, on a piece of cardboard, sat a bony old man with matted hair and a scruffy beard. He wore a black hooded sweatshirt with the words *Circle Line* printed in faded script on the front. One of his gnarled hands rested on a two-by-four that lay beside him.

"Who's that?" Jack whispered.

"Just the bum who hangs out here," Euri said. "Don't worry about him."

Jack looked at the homeless man, who didn't seem to register their conversation.

"Come on," said Euri. "I can show you the coolest thing of all on the other side of the canal."

But as they reached the edge of the canal, the homeless man suddenly glared at Jack and stuck out a bony hand.

"Old beggar," Euri said dismissively. She turned to Jack. "He's seen me before. But he seems to want something from you."

Jack reached into his pocket and dropped some change into the man's outstretched hand. The beggar looked at what Jack had given him, frowned, and threw the coins at him. Jack leaped backward.

Even Euri looked alarmed. "Don't you have something else to give him?"

"Like what?" Jack turned to the old man. "Do you want food? My jacket?"

The man continued to stare silently at him.

Jack dug into his pockets again and pulled out everything he could grasp. Dr. Lyons's token glittered among the lint and pennies and gum wrappers. He picked it out. It seemed a shame to give it away. But he didn't have anything else. He dropped it in the old man's palm.

The old man studied the token. Then he jumped to his feet with surprising agility, and before Jack could back away, hefted the two-by-four over his shoulder. Jack raised his hands to protect his head, but the old man turned away from him and slapped the wooden plank over the canal. Then he pointed to Jack and gestured for him to cross it.

VIII | Another World

Jack scurried across the two-by-four. When he turned around, Euri was standing behind him. The beggar, however, had disappeared. "Where did he go?" Jack asked.

"Probably to bother someone else. That wasn't so bad though, was it?"

Euri flashed him a new teacher's slightly too enthusiastic grin. Jack could tell that she was hiding something. He looked around, wondering exactly where he was. Again, the echoing cries poured down from the ceiling. "Where are those voices coming from?"

"We're at the bottom of the whispering gallery," Euri said. She pointed to the pillars. "The voices travel down here, and then they boomerang back up. Want to see more?"

But before he could answer, she held up her hand and cocked her ear. Jack listened too. Loud barks were echoing toward them from a passageway behind. "I thought you said there weren't dogs down here," Jack said.

"There's just one," said Euri. "We'd better go."

The barking sounded like it was coming from a chorus of dogs rather than just one, and it was growing louder. Jack looked at his watch. He was certain he had missed the next train and probably the one after that. But according to the watch, it was just 4:29 p.m., only fifteen minutes later than it had been when he had checked it in the whispering gallery. Jack tapped the watch's face, but the second hand failed to move. He pulled the cell phone his father had given him out of his backpack, but it also was dead. "Maybe I should go," Jack said. He turned back to the canal, and his stomach flip-flopped. The bridge was gone.

"You don't understand, do you?" Euri said in a tense whisper. "The guards will be here in seconds with that disgusting dog. If they think you're one of us trying to escape . . . We'd better . . ."

"Wait a second," Jack interrupted. "What do you mean, 'one of us'?"

Euri's eyes darted around the room.

"What are you?'" Jack demanded.

Euri pursed her lips and stared him straight in the face. "What am I?" she repeated, her voice rising. "How about who am I? Who! Just because I'm dead doesn't mean I've become a what!"

"Right," said Jack with a smile, "you're dead." But

Euri's sullen expression didn't change. He suddenly noticed how pale she was, how her uniform, with its prim-collared blouse and faded plaid skirt, looked outdated. The girl in front of him was dead. He took a step backward and nearly fell. No wonder she hadn't been afraid of being hit by the train—she was already in her grave. But it was hard to think of Euri as dead when she was standing in front of him with her arms crossed in front of her chest, looking just as alive as he did.

"Wait!" Jack said. "I'm not dead too, am I? A few days ago I was hit by a car, and then I woke up in the hospital. . . ."

Euri dismissively waved her hand. "That doctor said you were perfectly fine. And anyway, if you were dead you wouldn't wake up in a hospital. You'd wake up on the Circle Line." She looked away from him before quietly adding, "And you would be absolutely certain how you died."

"The Circle Line?"

"The ferry. If you were dead, you wouldn't cross over by bridge."

"Why didn't you tell me you were . . ." He paused, wondering if Euri would find the word polite. "A ghost?"

A particularly fierce-sounding bark made them both turn in the direction of the passageway. "It's not exactly an icebreaker, okay?" Euri whispered. "'Hi, I'm dead. Want to hang out?' I thought we'd get to know each other first. Ease into it. But listen, we can talk more about it later. The guards are coming, and if they find out you're alive . . . we've got to hide."

Jack studied Euri's wan face. It was hard to believe she was lying. "Okay. Where do we go?"

Euri ran into the passageway. "This way."

"But that's going toward them!"

"Just trust me!"

Jack didn't seem to have a choice. Euri ran ahead of him through the narrow dirt-walled passageway, and he followed close behind her. A rank animal smell drifted through. "What is that?" Jack whispered.

But instead of answering, Euri flung herself on her hands and knees. She pointed to a cranny in the wall. "In here!" she ordered. She slithered into it headfirst and disappeared.

Jack was suddenly alone. He looked at the hole, no bigger than an animal's burrow.

"Jack!" Euri whispered.

With a loud snarl, something bounded toward him.

IX | The New York Underworld

Jack dove into the tiny tunnel. Euri held her finger to her lips. Jack nodded and didn't make a sound.

Just a few feet away, four enormous paws paced back and forth. Strings of drool pooled to the ground. A huge black head darted into the tunnel entrance, and a pair of red eyes met Jack's. The dog bared its long, white teeth and began to bark. The smell that issued from its mouth made Jack's stomach turn. Then another head pushed its way into the entrance and began to bark. And another. Jack gasped. All three heads were attached to the same body. It was Cerberus, the supposedly mythical three-headed dog that guarded the underworld. Luckily, he was too large to fit the rest of his body into the tunnel.

"Heel!" a deep, male voice shouted in a New York accent. "Damned mutt. He's wedged in there so tight I can't see past him."

"Get up," ordered another voice—this one commanding and cold. "He always thinks he smells something in those little tunnels. There's no one there."

Two of the heads yelped, but the third snapped at Jack before it was yanked away.

Jack felt a tug on his jacket. Euri motioned to him to crawl deeper into the tunnel. Long, ropelike roots hung down from the brick walls, and beetles scampered over them. As he edged forward, his backpack scraping the top of the tunnel, he whispered, "Is this the Greek underworld?"

Euri shook her head. "Nah. It's the New York underworld. The Greek underworld's in Astoria."

"Astoria?"

"Yeah, Astoria, Queens. That's where all the Greeks live."

"If you're dead," said Jack, "how come I can see you?"

"Because you're in the underworld too now," Euri said. "The question is how you were able to see me before you crossed over. I've been hanging out in that station for seven years, and no one living ever has. You even convinced the old beggar to let you in. I didn't think he would."

"Charon," said Jack.

"Who?"

"The old beggar. His name is Charon. In Greek mythology, he's the gatekeeper to the underworld. He ferries the dead across the River Styx in exchange for coins.

That's why the ancient Greeks put coins in people's mouths after they died."

Euri shrugged. "You're in New York, not ancient Greece."

"Well, subway tokens, then. Are you sure I'm not dead?"

"You didn't find that token in your mouth, did you?"

She started to crawl forward, but Jack didn't follow her. "Are all the dead here?"

Euri turned around. "Not all the dead. Mostly just the ones who died in New York."

"My mother died in New York."

"I know. You told me."

Jack thought about his accident, how it had led him to New York, and to Euri. Maybe following her to track 61 hadn't been a mistake. Maybe it was meant to happen, so he could find his mother. For the first time in years he allowed himself to imagine seeing her again, and his chest tightened. He took a deep breath. "Do you think I could find her?"

"It depends on whether she's moved on yet."

Euri began to crawl forward, and this time Jack followed her. "Moved on?"

"Yes, to Elysium."

Jack knew that Elysium was the region of the underworld where heroes went after they died. It was supposed to be a peaceful place where the dead spent their days hunting and feasting. "Where is Elysium?" he asked.

"Somewhere in the Hamptons," said Euri. "That's my guess, anyway. But none of us really know because we haven't moved on yet. And it's impossible to contact anyone once they've gone there. They're supposed to be in this state of total peace, and they don't want ghosts who still have problems disrupting them."

Jack wanted to ask how the dead moved on to Elysium, but he was distracted by a shuffling sound up ahead. "What's that?"

"It's safer for you to hide in a crowd. Hopefully you'll blend in. So listen up. Here's your story. You died this morning. You were . . ."

"Hit by a train?" Jack offered.

"Good choice," said Euri with a snort. "Try not to look anyone in the eye for too long. There's something creepy about your eyes. They look alive."

"How do I find out if my mom's still here?" Jack asked.

"Well, we can start by just looking around," Euri said. Shoving furiously, she pushed her way out of the end of the tunnel. Jack couldn't tell what she was pushing against until she pulled him after her, and he found himself in a crowd of shadowy beings jammed into a wide, stone passageway. The ghostly procession slowly shuffled forward, carrying him and Euri along with it. Like Euri, the dead appeared no different from the living, except for their pale faces and their eyes, which were dull and translucent regardless of color. A few murmured to each other, but most were quiet and shared the anxious, preoccupied look of the living commuters eight stories above.

Jack panned their faces, hoping to recognize his mom. There were a number of old people, many of them in nightgowns, but also many younger people in a wide range of dress—knickers and flouncy shirts, police uniforms, Native American headdresses, elegant lace-trimmed gowns, turbans, jeans, tattered coats, saris, mink stoles, heavy black suits and hats, tweed caps, dirty smocks, silk Chinese suits, tuxedoes. There were children too—a few in sailor outfits or dresses, many more in rags.

"Even if she is down here, how am I going to find my mom?" he whispered to Euri. "It's packed!"

"Well, I thought maybe you'd just luck out," she whispered back. "But you're right. It's not so easy to find someone down here."

Jack frowned and went back to studying the crowd. The array of faces—every age, race, and ethnicity—stretched in every direction. "How do all these people fit down here?" Jack asked.

"They're spirits. They don't really take up any room at all."

Jack noted that Euri didn't include herself in the description, though she too was a ghost. "Euri?"

"Yes?"

"How'd you die?"

"'I died for beauty but was scarce/Adjusted in the tomb,'" said a man's voice in a Scottish brogue behind them.

Jack instantly recognized the lines of the poem and turned around. "'When one who died for truth was lain/In an adjoining room,'" he continued.

"Emily Dickinson," said the ghost, who had a white beard and a pipe hanging out of his mouth. "Fine stuff, though I prefer Blake myself."

The ghost continued to stare at Jack until his pipe sagged to the point of dropping out of his mouth.

"He's new," Euri said. "Just died this morning."

"Hit by a train," Jack added eagerly.

The man grunted. "Didn't mean to stare, lad. Thought there was something live about you. Welcome. Todd's the name, Ruthven—rhymes with livin' but spelled R-U-T-H-V-E-N, mind you, confusing for Americans, I know. I was an author, poet, and editor myself. You may have read my series of children's books—*Space Cat, Space Cat and the Kittens*?"

Jack shook his head. "Sorry."

"Oh, well," said Todd, trying to hide his disappointment.

"Not everyone is E. B. White. Anyway, lad, what's your name?"

"I'm . . ." Jack wondered whether to say his real name. "Jack?"

"Well then, Jack, it's nice that the young ghosts know some poetry today. We have a club of poets and the like that meets every night at the White Horse Tavern. You should drop by sometime. You might know a few. Two a.m."

Jack tried not to look confused. The endless expanse of stone passageways seemed unlikely to end in a bar. Two in the morning also seemed on the late side for a meeting.

"We'll see you later," Euri said, shoving through the crowd and steering Jack along with her. "Some of the dead can be very chatty," she remarked when they had left Todd.

"What was he talking about?" Jack asked as they pushed their way into a new group of ghosts. "Is there a tavern down here?"

"We'll get to that in a second," she whispered. "There's something else we need to worry about first."

"What?" asked Jack.

The crowd suddenly lurched forward. "Finally!" sniffed a gray-haired woman in a pillbox hat. Jack noticed that some of the ghosts were moving to the left, while others were moving to the right.

"Hold on," Euri said. "We'll need to sneak away at the last moment."

"The last moment before what?" Jack asked. But Euri ignored him and steered him to the left.

A series of barks rose over the shuffling sound. Euri froze. "The guards," she whispered. She shoved her way across the stream of ghosts to a tunnel that split off to the right. Jack tried to follow her, but several portly men in vests began shoving him in the opposite direction. For spirits that didn't take up any room at all, they felt surprisingly solid. "What a rabble!" one of them remarked.

Euri grabbed his hand. Hers was cold but surprisingly firm. As she tugged harder, he had to stop himself from crying out as his shoulder pulled in the socket. Finally, he slipped in between two of the portly men, and Euri dragged him into the tunnel. The surging crowd swept them forward. Up ahead, Jack saw tiny circles of pale light filtering down from the ceiling.

"You won't be able to get out this way," Euri whispered as she frantically tried to steer him in the opposite direction. "It won't work. We've got to turn back."

"What's going on?" Jack whispered. But Euri was too busy trying to pull him out of the flow of spirits to answer. "I can't . . ." she huffed as they were pushed forward past a red line on the dirt and under the circles of light. A spirit in a Yankees baseball cap counted them with a clicker. "Have a nice trip," he said mechanically. "See you at dawn."

Euri's hand tightened around his own. Before Jack even had a chance to cry out, he felt himself rising toward the tiny circles. His body stretched until it was as thin as a wire and began to spiral up through greenish-gray copper pipes. He felt Euri's fingers slip away. He opened his mouth and tried to shout, but he couldn't make a sound.

X | The Angel of the Waters

Euri's hand closed back around his, and with a loud pop, Jack felt his body shoot out of the pipe and fly up into the cold, winter air like a champagne cork. His eyes widened as he caught sight of the snow-covered ground some twenty feet below. He gripped Euri's hand as tightly as he could and frantically flapped his free arm and legs.

"That was great!" exclaimed Euri, who was floating calmly beside him. "You actually made it through." She leaned over and peered into his eyes. "They still look alive. Relax. You're not going to fall."

Slowly, Jack stopped jerking his limbs. He tried not to look down. "Why am I not falling?"

"I don't know," Euri admitted. "Maybe because we're holding hands. We were holding hands when you went through the fountain too. Let's test it." She began to loosen her fingers.

"No!" Jack squeaked as he tightened his grip on her hand.

"Okay, relax," Euri said. "You're clearly alive, because you're so afraid of death. It's probably the hand-holding. That must be how you're able to do the normal ghost things."

"What are the normal ghost things?"

"Shuffle through dark passages, moan, rattle chains." Euri chuckled at her own joke. "You'll see," she said. "The ghost powers will make our search for your mom a little easier. In the meantime, enjoy the view."

Jack looked around. Spindly trees were silhouetted against a darkening sky. Beneath him was a three-tiered bronze fountain. He felt a strange sense of déjà vu. "I know this place," he said.

Euri shrugged. "I'm not surprised. It's Bethesda Terrace, one of the most popular spots in Central Park."

"No, that fountain. My mother took me here a few days before she died. She was staring at it."

Jack stared at it himself. On top of it was a statue of a winged angel. From tiny holes beneath her feet, ghosts were streaming out. Hundreds of them burst into the air and unfurled themselves, shaking out kinks and wrinkles like sheets in the wind. Although many of them were dressed in flimsy nightgowns and light shirts, they didn't seem to feel the cold. Instantly, some flew away, skirting the tops of trees, hurrying toward the city skyline. Others zoomed up and down in what

Jack guessed was their own version of aerobics.

"The dead come out here every night at dusk," Euri explained. "And not just here but at other fountains around the city too. But, like I said, it's a pretty popular place for the living too. Your mom was probably just looking at the statue, the Angel of the Waters."

"She seemed upset," said Jack.

"Well, that's good. It means she probably hasn't moved on yet. It usually takes ghosts a while to move on if they have a lot of issues from their life they need to work out." Euri paused and looked out across the frozen park toward the city. Jack was certain that she was thinking about her own issues, but it didn't seem like the right time to ask.

"Did your mom seem unhappy a lot?" she asked.

Jack thought for a moment. "Except for that one time, I don't really remember. My father won't talk about her."

"You don't have any older brothers or sisters who remember?"

"No," said Jack. "I'm an only child."

Euri grinned. "Really? Me too."

"That must be hard on your parents."

Euri stared at him blankly. Jack rushed to explain, "I mean, your being dead."

As soon as he had finished speaking, Jack wished he could take the words back. Euri's mouth twitched. "I thought we were talking about *your* parents," she said.

Jack nodded, relieved to change the subject. "Right. My dad won't talk about my mom."

Euri balanced her chin in her hand and assumed a studious look. "Maybe they didn't get along?"

Jack felt annoyed. "No, that's not it. He just misses her."

"Did he say that?" asked Euri.

"No, but—"

"The important thing now," she interrupted, "is that we need a clue, something that will help us find her if she's still here. Do you have anything that was hers—a half-written letter, a journal?"

Jack started to shake his head but then stopped and reached behind him to pull Egbert Viele's map out of his backpack. "I think I saw a ghost in my father's office yesterday. He jumped out the window before I could talk to him, but he left this behind."

"So I'm not the first spirit you've seen?" Euri asked as she took the map. She sounded a little disappointed.

"I didn't know he was a ghost," Jack said; but as soon as Euri opened up the map, her face brightened.

"Hey look! It's a map of the underworld rivers. Here's the one you crossed." With her finger, she traced the circle of rivers around Grand Central Terminal. "But what does this have to do with your mother?"

Jack pointed to the handwritten scrawl. "Anastasia.

That's her name. It's written in my father's hand-writing."

"That's strange. Why has your father written her name on an underworld map? And why did this ghost leave it for you?"

"I'm not sure he left it for me," Jack corrected. "I think he took it from my father's desk drawer to look at, himself. I think I just frightened him, and he dropped it. I wanted to know who he was."

"Well, who could blame him? It's pretty scary when a living person can see you and demands to know who you are."

"You didn't seem afraid," Jack said.

"Yes, but I'm different," Euri explained. "I'm comfortable with the living."

Jack was tempted to remind her that he was the only living person who had ever seen her, but he felt they were getting away from the subject of his mother. "So you think this map is a clue?"

"It's our only one," announced Euri, handing it back to him. "We need to find out more about it."

"How are we going to do that?"

"My friend Professor Schmitt. He would have been alive when this map was made. He may be able to tell us more."

The shrill barking of a dog startled Jack. Beneath him,

he spotted a little yellow terrier looking up and barking furiously. A living man bundled up in a sheepskin jacket was tugging on the dog's leash. "Come on, Abbie!"

"He'll see us!" Jack whispered.

But Euri just laughed. "He can't see us or hear us, either. We're invisible. That's another ghost thing. And anyway, he's a New Yorker. He probably won't even look up."

Just as Euri predicted, the man continued to peer absently down at the snow while yanking the little dog. "Shush, Abbie!" he murmured. "Shush! There's nothing there."

"Quiet!" Euri shouted. The little dog whimpered and stopped barking. Euri turned to Jack. "We'll watch the end of the sunset," she said. "And then we'll go."

As though a giant valve were slowly closing, the stream of ghosts that issued from the fountain slowed to a trickle. The man and his dog left the fountain and disappeared. The park began to grow dark. One by one, lights twinkled on. Euri seemed lost in thought. With his free hand, Jack replaced the map and pulled the cell phone out of his backpack. It was still dead. He couldn't help feeling relieved—he didn't relish the prospect of explaining to his father that he was still in New York and had missed the train, not to mention that he was flying around with a ghost.

Euri finally pointed to the city lights, sparkling on the east side of the park. "Ready to go?"

Jack nodded and with a shake of Euri's ponytail, they flew toward the tall buildings on Fifth Avenue.

XI | The Haunted Penthouse

In the beginning, they flew low enough for Jack to touch the tops of the trees with his feet. But as they neared the edge of the park, Euri began to steer them higher and higher. "The best views of the city are aerial ones," she explained. Jack's stomach dropped as the wind whipped against his face. "Look down!" Euri shouted. "Isn't this fun?"

Fifteen stories below, Fifth Avenue was a dizzying sight. Tiny taxis honked and toy-size buses rumbled. People the size of dolls dashed across the street as hundreds of ghosts flew over their heads. "Pretty cool," Jack admitted. "But are you sure I won't fall?"

Euri chuckled. "Of course not!"

Jack clutched her hand tighter. They sailed across Fifth Avenue and skirted the side of an elegant apartment building with stone garlands and cornucopias carved into its facade. Through windows where the drapes were open, Jack could see apartments decorated with oil paintings, chandeliers, and heavy, dark furniture. A number of ghosts floated just outside the windows, watching the people inside. "Haunters," Euri explained.

"Don't you haunt?" Jack asked.

Euri made a face. "Nah."

Jack watched a balding ghost in a tailored suit gaze longingly at someone inside an apartment. He thought about his mom. "They must miss the people they haunt," he said.

Euri scowled. "Maybe. But I bet the living aren't even thinking about them."

"I'm sure they think about them a lot," Jack said defensively. Hardly a day went by when he didn't think about his mother. Euri didn't give the living any credit. "Why did you start talking to me, anyway, in Grand Central?"

Euri gave him a funny look. "I wasn't trying to contact you in particular. You were just the first person who could hear me."

"But why were you trying to talk to living people? That's haunting, isn't it? Don't you have any dead friends to talk to?" Jack realized that he was being rude, but he couldn't stop himself. "I mean, aren't there better things to do than hang out in Grand Central all night?"

Jack thought Euri would get mad, but instead she looked uncomfortable. "I'm not a haunter."

He gave her a skeptical look.

"Look," she said crossly, "haunting isn't like what we're doing now. It's not like you get to hang out and talk. It's one-sided. Here, I'll show you."

Euri shot up to a penthouse window and hovered outside it. "Take a look."

Inside the apartment, on a finely upholstered couch, sat a silver-haired man and a stately blond woman reading a book to a small Asian girl in red pajamas, who sat in between them. A fire crackled in the fireplace, and in the corner of the room stood an enormous Christmas tree decorated in white lights, a silver star on top grazing the ceiling. Jack had almost forgotten that just days ago it had been Christmas—he and his father had celebrated it with a scraggly tree they'd bought on Christmas Eve and a few practical gifts. But in a living room the size of Jack's entire apartment was the Christmas he had always imagined— outsize stockings, big red nutcrackers, silver bowls of peppermints, garlands of pine and sprigs of mistletoe, knee-high piles of books and toys under the tree. A small white dog slept by the fire, and a maid crocheted in the corner. The little girl looked up to the woman and said something, and both she and the man laughed.

Euri hurled herself at the closed window and Jack shut his eyes, expecting to smack into the glass like a bird. But instead, the air turned warm; and when he opened his

eyes, he was floating with Euri inside the penthouse.
"Merry Christmas!" Euri shouted at the family. Then she
began singing "Silent Night" at the top of her lungs.

Jack froze, half expecting the entire family to turn
around and scream at the sight of Euri standing in the
middle of their living room. The pallor of her skin was
gray, and angry strands of hair had loosened from her
ponytail and were poking up around her face. But the
family took no notice of her or of Jack.

Only the maid looked out the window and into
the night with a slightly worried expression. "The Van-
dermeers' holiday party is tonight," she remarked.

Euri started in on the second verse. " 'Shepherds quake
at the sight,' " she screeched.

The blond woman looked up. She had a long, elegant
face that, without a smile, made her look as imperious as
a statue. "We haven't gone in at least five years," she said.
"I suppose we should go."

The little girl jumped off the couch and began to
dance next to Jack. "No, no, no, no-o-o-o-o-o!" she said,
hopping from one foot to the other. "Don't go!"

The silver-haired man laughed and turned to the
woman. "Quite a show. What do you say, Mom?"

"I didn't really want to go, anyway." The woman
smiled and held out her arms. "Okay, Janie. We'll stay
with you."

"'SLEEP IN HEAVENLY PEACE!'" shrieked Euri. With a final whoop, she flew at the window, pulling Jack back through it and onto the ledge. She stood there for a quiet moment, the wind whipping through her hair, her back turned to the cozy scene in the penthouse. "See," she finally said, "that's haunting for you. Pretty boring. Let's go."

"Did you know those people?" Jack asked.

Euri gave a hollow-sounding chuckle. "Nah. First time I've seen them in my death."

Euri dove off the ledge, yanking Jack with her. He didn't believe her. He wanted to ask more questions, but could tell from the way that she avoided his gaze that the conversation was over. He regretted pushing her to haunt. Her mood had turned sour. She began to fly faster than before, dipping between buildings and then hurtling over the rooftops. She kept her face turned away from his.

"We're almost there," she said at last, pointing to an enormous marble building with a Beaux Arts facade of columns and arches. Two giant stone lions guarded the entrance.

"The New York Public Library," she announced as they began to descend.

They gently glided down to the sidewalk. Jack was surprised to see dozens of ghosts, some in colonial vests and wigs, others in flapper dresses, still others in T-shirts and jeans, floating down the sidewalk alongside the living. "What if they bump into each other?" he asked.

Euri's pale eyes narrowed. "Watch this." Pulling him along, she ran straight at a living policeman who was talking into his radio. Jack cringed, but they went right through him. The policeman shivered and yanked up the zipper of his jacket.

"Fur is evil!" she shouted, running into a woman in a mink coat as she scurried to catch a taxi. A slight frown crossed the woman's face, but she continued to run. "See?"

"They seemed to sense something, though," Jack remarked.

"Some do, but it's just a mood, a blast of warm or cold, a memory, that's all."

Pulling him after her, she bounded in gentle floating arcs up the stairs to the library. A sign outside announced the library's hours as 10–6. A living guard was chaining a padlock to the door.

"Looks like they just opened up," Euri said as she pulled him through the closed door.

XII | Regulation 41.5a

They entered a marble chamber that blazed with the light of hundreds of electric candles mounted on stone candelabras. As soon as Jack's eyes adjusted, he noticed the dead. They were everywhere: floating ten feet up in the air, arms filled with books, hanging off the onion-shaped brass chandeliers as they read, flying absently back and forth as they fluttered through the pages of yellowing newspapers. On the left side of the entrance was an information booth manned by a floating white-haired librarian who was busily scribbling into a ledger. Posted to the front of his desk was a printed sign. It read:

There are many requests for assistance in researching "the occult," as it is popularly called, particularly from the recently dead. While the New York Public Library has an extensive collection on such topics as divination and the Russian mystic H. P. Blavatsky, we request that you first attend a "Now That You're Dead" seminar before seeking further information on these or other "occult" topics.

Sincerely,

Wilberforce Eames, Bibliographer

"What's a 'Now That You're Dead' seminar?" Jack asked, pointing to the sign.

Euri rolled her eyes, but the librarian closed his ledger and stood up from his chair. "You must be right off the boat," he said with a kindly smile. "Float on up, young man. You'll see. They should be just beginning."

Euri hurried Jack toward a pair of marble staircases. "I suppose we have to go past the McGraw Rotunda anyway. You might as well listen in."

They drifted up the left staircase, which gently spiraled upward till it met the right in a high, arched anteroom. About thirty ghosts, most of them old, and all of them dressed in modern-day clothing, stood meekly beneath colorful ceiling murals. A few whispered in groups, but the majority silently looked up at the murals. Jack and Euri joined them. Each mural, Jack noticed, depicted someone reading or writing—Moses explaining the Ten Commandments, a monk inscribing a scroll, a man poring over the page of a printing press, a newsboy in colonial-era breeches hawking a paper. After a while, Euri pulled Jack up so that they were floating beneath the mural of the ancient Greek god Prometheus stealing the knowledge of fire from the gods and giving it to men. "This one's my favorite," Euri declared in a voice too loud for a library.

But before Jack could shush her, a recording of chamber music boomed through invisible speakers and the candelabras and chandeliers flickered. The rest of the ghosts looked around expectantly. To Jack's relief, Euri floated back down and assumed a serious expression. The haunting strains of a clavichord softened into a backdrop as a high-pitched male voice bleated over the speakers. "Elegant. Mysterious. Timeless," he intoned, pausing for a measure of violin music. "Death."

Euri clapped her hand over her mouth as her shoulders shook with laughter. Jack was torn between elbowing Euri in the side and laughing along with her.

"For thousands of years, people just like you have joined in this age-old tradition."

"Tradition?" Euri whispered.

"Shhh!" said a man in a hospital gown behind her.

"I'm Fiorello LaGuardia, former mayor of New York, and on behalf of the New York Public Library and the City of New York, I'd like to welcome you to the afterlife and share some tips for making your stay eternally pleasant."

"Or just eternal," whispered Euri.

The chandeliers went dark as an image of a ghost

a briefcase flying out of a fountain was projected in front of them. "I'm a New York ghost," he said, tipping a fedora in their direction. Next the camera panned a long line of living Rockettes, and then stopped and held on a ghost Rockette high-kicking along with them at the end. "I'm a New York ghost," she brayed. A taxicab splashed through a puddle near Times Square, and a ghost in a fez poked his head out of the back window. "I'm a New York ghost," he shouted with a proud grin. A shot of the Circle Line ferry passing the Statue of Liberty, the deck packed with waving ghosts, followed as a voice-over of the three ghosts declared in unison, "We're New York ghosts! And we're proud to welcome you to the New York underworld!"

"Definitely Oscar-worthy," Euri remarked.

As postcard images of ghosts holding up beer steins, flying through the Plaza Hotel, and wrapping themselves coyly in bolts of cloth in the Garment District flashed in front of them, LaGuardia began to talk. "New York ghosts come in all shapes, races, ages, and sizes. We're a diverse afterlife community. But we all have one thing in common —we love the New York underworld!"

"Rah, rah," said Euri flatly.

"If you died in New York, you automatically received citizenship from its first-class underworld," LaGuardia continued. "If you had the misfortune to die elsewhere, but resided in the city during a formative period of your life, you can still join us by applying for perpetual residency."

A relieved-looking ghost in a "New Jersey Girl" T-shirt proudly held up her New York underworld residency card.

"In your afterlife, you'll enjoy several powers—flying, invisibility, and transmobility—or the ability to move through solid objects such as doors, windows, and walls. Flying is often a challenge for new ghosts, but the city offers free lessons at the Thirtieth Street heliport."

An image of a dozen ghosts flying shakily in a line over the heliport flashed in the air.

"At night, the city is yours to roam. You will probably find that you will choose to stay in the neighborhoods you frequented during your life, but you can travel anywhere on the island of Manhattan. Keep in mind, however, that you cannot fly over water."

A shot of a ghost crash-landing at the end of a pier appeared in front of them.

"Haunting is a popular afterlife activity. You are welcome to haunt your living friends or family during the evening hours, but please do not attempt to contact them by participating in séances or other occult rites."

A still shot of a ghost moving a man's hand on a Ouija board was marked over with a big red X.

"That stuff is so phony, anyway," whispered Euri.

"At dawn, you must return to the subterranean under-world by one of the approximately fifty fountains in New York. One of our friendly spirit counters will register both your exit at dusk and your return at dawn."

A ghost in a Yankees cap held up his clicker for the camera.

"We saw that guy!" Jack whispered.

"If you attempt to stay aboveground during daylight hours, the spirit counters will notice that you have not returned and alert our security team. These skilled and seasoned guards are trained to immediately escort guests belowground who have lingered past dawn above-ground."

This was followed by a black-and-white photo of the underworld guards standing in a stiff school-photo like line, with Cerberus in front of them. They were a rough-looking bunch with thick necks and enormous fists. But the one Jack found most menacing was a tall, bullet-headed ghost with a bushy mustache and flat blue eyes. He wore a double-breasted black uniform and stood slightly in the foreground, one hand gripping the scruff of Cerberus's middle neck, the other a nightstick.

"New arrivals often ask why they have to return belowground during the day," the mayor cheerfully con-tinued. "To answer that question we've prepared this short segment on the dangers of staying past dawn."

The word REENACTMENT flashed onto the screen in red letters as a shot of the sunrise gave way to a close-up of a greasy-haired ghost sneaking away from a fountain. As the sun rose, he began to grow paler. His fingers started to disappear and then one of his arms. "Help!" he tried to shout, but the word was cut off as his mouth disappeared. In the next scene, as an alarm wailed, two of the burly guards, wearing what looked like hazmat suits, flew out of the fountain. Grasping the ghost by his remaining arm, they dragged him back into the underworld.

"Sometimes the dead stay out past dawn under the misimpression that they will be able to live again," the mayor said in a stern voice when the clip ended. "We'd like to remind you that you cannot live again, and it's a serious offense to attempt it by any means. Rule breakers will be punished to the fullest extent of the law. So if you, or a ghost you know, talks about living again or attempting to live again, we encourage you to call 1-800-END-LIFE before it's too late. Professional help is available."

Jack looked at Euri, expecting her to make a joke, but she was silently picking at her skirt.

The classical music faded out and was replaced by the sound of waves crashing on a beach. LaGuardia's voice became solemn. "One day, when you have resolved all the problems that troubled you during your life, your stay with us will come to an end. You will move on to

Elysium, the realm of eternal peace and happiness."

"ELYSIUM!" chanted a chorus of disembodied voices over the crash of the waves. One of the ghosts in the audience sighed.

"In the meantime," said the mayor, "we want to assure you that the New York underworld protects you from acquiring new problems after death. Although you may hear stories about the living venturing into the underworld and creating new problems for the dead, these are only stories. No living person has ever entered into this realm."

Jack turned to Euri. She shifted uneasily.

The ocean noises faded away and the classical music resumed. "Once again, we'd like to thank you for choosing to die in the greatest city on earth."

As a final montage of New York ghosts giving the thumbs-up flashed in front of them, and the violins struck up in an ear-piercing finale, several of the ghosts broke into awkward applause. Then the speakers went dead, the lights flickered back on, and everyone seemed at a loss. A little old ghost with a wisp of white hair jutting from his head and a pair of wire-frame glasses shuffled into the rotunda. "Okay, movie over," he grumbled. "Any questions?"

"Ask him what they'd do to a liv . . . you know, a person like me." Jack whispered.

"No!" Euri said.

Jack knew it was something bad—Cerberus hadn't exactly wanted to play fetch with him. "I'll ask myself, then."

Jack started to raise his hand, but Euri yanked it back down. "They'll figure out who you are. . . ."

"No questions? Everyone know everything?" the old ghost asked the crowd.

"Then ask for me," Jack pleaded. "You're the one who led me here."

He made a motion to raise his hand. "Okay!" Euri hissed, quickly raising her own.

The old ghost squinted at her through his glasses. "A question, okay. What is it?"

"I know that no living person has ever gotten into the underworld but, uh, what would happen to them if they did?"

The old ghost shook his head so that his wisp of white hair waved. "You've heard too many stories, young girl. Never happens."

"Yes, but . . . but what if it did happen?"

The old ghost sighed and pulled a small, well-worn book out of his front pocket. "Live people coming in," he muttered, flipping through the pages. "Okay, let me see. Flight accidents and liability; maximum occupancy of fountains . . . Aha. Here it is." He stopped flipping and began to read aloud as he traced his finger down the page. "'Regulation 41.5a. No living person has ever entered into the realm of the dead. But if they did, they would be fed to the flesh-eating three-headed dog that guards the underworld.'"

Jack swallowed so loudly that he was certain everyone heard. But the rest of the ghosts didn't seem to notice. The old ghost slammed the handbook shut, which released a small cloud of dust. "Any other questions?"

When no one answered he drifted off. The rest of the recently dead began to file out of the rotunda, several attempting short bouts of flight. "So," Euri said when they'd left, "feel better now?"

Jack glared at her. "You knew about the guards and the dog, what they would do to me. You knew, and you still had me come."

Euri looked hurt. "I've given you an opportunity. You said you wanted to find your mother. There's still a good chance you can. Come on, Jack. And besides, except for your eyes, you really look like one of us."

"Thanks," he said gloomily.

She squeezed his hand. "Come on, let's go see Professor Schmitt. He'll help you find your mom."

But as she led him out of the rotunda, Jack swore he heard Cerberus's paws tapping on the marble floor.

XIII | Professor Schmitt's Secret

They floated into a catalog room, past a living guard tipped back in his chair asleep, and toward another door. Above it, Jack noticed an inscription: A GOOD BOOKE IS THE PRECIOUS LIFE-BLOOD OF A MASTER SPIRIT, IMBALM'D AND TREASUR'D UP ON PURPOSE TO A LIFE BEYOND LIFE. They passed through a wood-paneled foyer and then turned right into an enormous room. Hundreds of the dead sat at rows of tables quietly reading. Dozens of others hovered just under a ceiling mural of billowing clouds blowing across a blue sky.

"They think they have light deprivation," Euri said, gesturing toward several who seemed to be sunning themselves.

She pointed to the other end of the reading room. "Professor Schmitt's usually at the back."

As they passed over rows of tables, Jack noticed a cadre of ghost librarians sailing up to a balcony filled with bookshelves and then zooming down to drop books into the hands of readers. A short ghost with a handlebar mustache caught one of them, opened it up, and pointed to the first page. "See here!" he cried, handing it to a skinny, big-toothed ghost who reminded Jack of a horse. "The latest copyright date is this year. I'm still in print."

"So what?" said the horsey-looking ghost. "The important thing is the last time someone took you out. Look, no one's checked out your book. Someone checked out mine last week. You're not exactly flying off the shelves, old boy."

The handlebar mustache grew red in the face. "This generation fails to appreciate me, is all."

Euri rolled her eyes at the two writers. "Too bad their egos didn't die with them."

Jack laughed, but he felt a little sorry for the handlebar mustache.

"Professor Schmitt's not like the others," Euri mused aloud. "He reads other people's books, new writers. Even though he died over a century ago, he's . . . I don't know . . . less dead."

"Why hasn't he moved on yet?" Jack asked.

Euri shrugged. "Some people move on almost as soon as they get here. For others it takes a long time. They're waiting."

"For what?"

"An answer that allows them to move on, or . . ." Euri's

voice drifted off. "Look," she said, "there's Professor Schmitt." She pointed to the farthest table in the room, where a white-haired ghost hovered just above his chair, tracing the lines of a book with his finger. "He knows eight languages," she said in a voice as reverential as Jack had heard her use.

As they floated down to the table, he noticed that Professor Schmitt's spine was bent. "He's a hunchback," Euri whispered. "If Elysium is fair, he'll be six feet tall."

"What did you say he taught when he was alive?"

"Classics, I think."

A fellow Classics scholar—certainly Professor Schmitt would help him find his mother. But before Jack could say anything, Euri flew over to the old man and touched him gently on his deformed back. "Professor Schmitt?"

The professor looked up from his book. His neck was long and gave him the appearance of a turtle poking out of its shell. "Euri, my dear! The most beautiful girl in the underworld. *Voulez-vous parler en français?*"

"*Non, merci, professeur.* I want to introduce you to someone. *Mon ami* Jack."

The professor shifted so that he was facing Jack. His pale gray eyes studied Jack's for several seconds. "Euri, how did you meet this young man?" he finally asked.

"Oh, I just met him after he got off the Circle Line. He died this morning. . . ."

"I'm a, was a, Latin scholar," Jack added, trying to change the subject. "I was translating the *Metamorphoses* before I died. But *tempus edax rerum*. Time devours all things," he said, translating the phrase for Euri.

"*Omnia tempus revelat,*" said Professor Schmitt.

Time reveals all things. Did the professor know he was alive?

But the old man smiled kindly and patted the seats next to him. "Euri, as you might guess from her name, is a great fan of the Orpheus myth," he said. "We read it together in French a few years ago. What can I help you children with?"

Jack pulled the Viele map out of his backpack and handed it to him.

"We're trying to find Jack's mother—if she hasn't moved on yet," Euri explained. "Just before Jack died he found this map of the underworld rivers with her name on it. We think it's a clue. We're hoping you can tell us something about it."

Professor Schmitt opened the map and flattened it out. "Aha," he said. "This wasn't meant to be a map of the underworld rivers, Euri. It's Mr. Viele's water map." He traced the green streams with his finger and then coughed gently as if beginning a lecture. "In my century, the city of New York was growing at a fast rate. There wasn't enough fresh water in those days, and the drinking water was often polluted and carried diseases like cholera and malaria. Viele was an engineer. He felt that builders needed to be more responsible where they built, so as to not contaminate the water supply. So he studied all the maps and drawings ever made of Manhattan, and from them he constructed this master map showing all the streams and rivers that ever existed on the island—both those above the surface and those underground. It's the only map showing Manhattan as it was when only Indians lived here, when it was just hills, marshes, and trout streams."

"What would a living person use it for today?" asked Jack.

"I've been told by newer ghosts that builders still use the Viele map to decide where to put down foundations for new buildings, to check whether they'll be prone to flooding. So a lot of people probably have this map. I'm not sure what it can tell you about your mother."

Euri looked disappointed. "So there's nothing unusual about it?"

Professor Schmitt looked around him and then lowered his voice. "Well, there is something I've heard."

"What?" Euri and Jack whispered in unison.

"Let's talk away from here." Jack and Euri followed Professor Schmitt over to a secluded corner of the reading room.

"There are those who say that the living have used this map to help them break into the underworld," he whispered, staring at Jack. "The Viele map shows all the rivers and streams, the ones that no longer exist, the ones that are dead. But those streams and rivers still exist in the underworld. There are stories that say if the living cross them, they can sneak in."

"I thought that's never happened," Jack interrupted. "In the 'Now That You're Dead' seminar they told us—"

"—the official line," said Professor Schmitt, handing him back the map. "There are reasons why they don't want the dead to believe that it's possible for the living to come in and contact them. For one, it would make it harder for them to move on if they thought a living person might break in and find them. Accepting death—and the end of contact with the living—is an essential step to moving on."

Jack's mouth felt dry. His father had the Viele map. Perhaps he had just been working on a dig that involved knowing where all the city's water sources were. But why then was his mother's name on the map? It seemed more likely that his father had been one of those living people—that he had sneaked into the underworld to visit his mother after she died. This would have made it harder for her to move on. "So all that the living need in order to sneak in is this map?" Jack asked.

"Oh no," said Professor Schmitt. "They'd have to have a golden bough as well."

"A golden what?" asked Euri.

"The golden bough," said Jack. "It's what allows Aeneas, the founder of Rome, to visit his dead father. When Charon, the ferryman, sees that Aeneas has the golden bough, he lets him into the underworld."

"Very good, Jack," said Professor Schmitt. He pulled a small book out of his pocket and handed it to him. *"Scientia est potentia."*

"Knowledge is power," Jack translated. The book was a thin volume with a cloth binding and no title on the cover or spine. He opened it up. *The Unofficial Guide to the New York Underworld* was handwritten on the first page.

"This will help answer your questions," Professor Schmitt explained. "Read it and make sure you stay as far away as you can from Clubber."

But before Jack had a chance to ask who Clubber was, the hall echoed with snarls. Jack looked over his shoulder. Two enormous guards were standing at the front of the reading room, the three-headed dog lunging on its chain. "I hate that dog," said Euri. She smiled but took a step back, pulling Jack with her. "We better go."

"Wait," said Professor Schmitt, handing him back the map. "There is a way to find out if your mother's still here and where you might find her, if that's why you came. When did she die?"

"Eight years ago."

"He smells something," one of the guards shouted.

"We really need to go," said Euri. She yanked Jack toward a small door at the back of the reading room marked EMERGENCY EXIT, 5TH AVENUE.

"Wait!" Jack cried, dragging her back to Professor Schmitt. "How do I find her?"

The guards began to march down the aisle toward them. Two of Cerberus's three mouths were frothing.

"There are records, Jack, of everyone here. Talk to Edna Gammon. She keeps the ones for that year. She haunts the St. James . . ."

But before Jack could catch the next word, Euri yanked him backward. He passed through the wooden emergency exit door, and his hand slipped from Euri's. Clutching the book, he fell back, tumbling down a flight of stairs.

XIV | The Unofficial Guide

Jack closed his eyes and waited for his head to crack against the marble stairs. But instead of hitting the landing, he felt himself jerk to a stop a few inches above it. Then Euri grabbed his hand again, and the air changed from musty and warm to crystalline cold. Opening his eyes, Jack realized that he was outside. The library was hundreds of feet below.

"It's okay," Euri said. "I got you."

"That was weird," Jack exclaimed.

"What was?"

"I felt like I floated. . . ."

"That's because I grabbed you. Good thing for you I'm fast."

Jack didn't want to argue, but several seconds before Euri had grabbed him, he felt as if he had hovered on his own. His thoughts were interrupted by a gust of wind. Jack looked down and realized that they were higher than they'd been before. Euri was making ascending loops around a skyscraper with a pointy steel top lit up like a torch. "Where are we going?" he asked.

"The Chrysler Building," she said. They landed on the outstretched neck of one of the steel eagles that jutted from the building's corners. The city below them was no longer made of steel and concrete but of a million white lights. Jack could see across it to the Empire State Building, its top floors and antenna dressed in holiday reds and greens, and beyond, to the dark expanse of New York Harbor. He tried to imagine the thousands of people eating and arguing and sleeping and working below. But this high up, except for the occasional gust of wind, it was quiet, and he couldn't quite believe anyone else existed in Manhattan but Euri and him. He looked at her and realized that she had been watching him. "I could stay here forever," he said.

Euri grimaced. "And it wouldn't change a bit. This isn't life." She pointed down at the city. "*That's* life."

Jack didn't bother to look. "That's having no friends at school and your mother being dead. . . ." He suddenly stopped. He had never said this to anyone.

Euri sighed. "At least it's life." She shook her head and pulled him down to sit on the eagle's neck. "Come on, let's take a look at that book."

Jack propped open the *Unofficial Guide* and they bent over the first page. Euri pointed to an inscription below the title and read it aloud. "'This volume has been compiled by truth seekers who shall go unnamed. *Felix qui potuit rerum cognoscere causas.*'"

"That's Latin, right? What does it mean?"

"'Happy is he who could know the cause of all things,'" Jack said. "It's Virgil."

He turned a few more pages until he reached the table of contents, which was also handwritten. He glanced at a few of the chapter titles: Now That You're Really Dead, The Real Truth about the Occult, Confessions of an Ex-Guard, Living Visitors to the Underworld. "Let's take a look at that last one," he said.

Euri flipped to the chapter and began to read aloud as Jack looked on. "'One of our favorite bits of misinformation from the Now That You're Dead seminar concerns living visitors to the underworld. Contrary to regulation 41.5a, from time to time the living have ventured into the world of the dead. And rather than create more problems for the dead, often they are destined to help them.

"'In order to enter into the underworld, the living must possess a golden bough. This bough may take the form of any object (see Henry Luce Adams's fascinating case study "The Golden Pastrami Sandwich") but will only appear golden to the person fated to have it.'"

"The subway token I gave Charon," Jack explained to Euri. "That was my golden bough."

Euri nodded. "I guess you're destined to be here, then."

"Destined to help my mom. Keep reading."

"'Egbert Viele's Sanitary and Topographical Map of the City and Island of New York is also recommended as a topographical guide to the underworld. There are also five other . . .'"

"Wait," Jack interrupted. "You skipped a line."

"'However,'" she read, "'as the regulation correctly states, living visitors to the underworld are in constant danger of being caught and destroyed by Cerberus.'"

Jack gave her a fierce look, but Euri just shrugged. "Well, we already knew that."

"Is there anything there about Clubber?" Jack asked, remembering the professor's warning.

Euri shook her head. "Not that I see." She kept on reading. "'There are also five other rules that govern their visits:

"'1) Like the dead, after dusk, living visitors to the New York underworld can remain belowground or venture above it (going aboveground, however, will not return them to the living world—see rule five for information on return trips). While in either place, living visitors can see and be seen by the dead and are invisible to the living. They also can engage in transmobility and flight, *but only if physically assisted by one of the dead.*

"'2) Living visitors should refrain from eating and drinking while visiting the New York underworld.

EVEN IF THEY FIND THEMSELVES AT AN IMPOSSIBLE-TO-RESERVE RESTAURANT. The smallest bite of fricassee of frog legs or sip of pomegranate martini can lead to a permanent stay.

"'3) Past visits are no guarantee of future returns. A golden bough is good for one, and only one, entry. The living should not assume that because they have found a golden bough once that they will be able to find another one repeatedly and at will.

"'4) The New York underworld is not responsible for lost items—including watches, cell phones, wallets, and other valuables, such as minds and spouses. If a living person leaves behind any of these during his visit, he should abandon all hope that he will ever get them back.

"'5) And most important of all, the only way for living visitors to return to the living world is through their original port of entry. Return trips are valid any day or night, except if a living person has stayed in the underworld for more than three nights. After this time, the strain of death on the living body becomes too much, and the visitor will be unable to return to the world of the living.'"

"Three nights?" said Jack. "I'm not going to stay that long."

"You could, though, if you wanted," said Euri.

Jack ignored her. "What I still don't understand is why I was able to see you in Grand Central. According to the guide, I shouldn't have seen you until I crossed into the underworld."

"You already had your golden bough," said Euri. "Maybe it gave you special powers."

"But I saw other ghosts before I found it."

Euri frowned. "I thought it was just *one* other."

"I think I saw a couple at the hospital after I woke up."

"Well, I'm glad the whole underworld's met you by now!"

Jack rushed to reassure her. "You're the first one I talked to. The rest of them seemed too scared."

This was a little bit of a lie—the ghosts in the hospital hadn't even seen him—but Euri looked pleased to hear it. "I told you most ghosts aren't good with the living," she said.

Jack closed the *Unofficial Guide* and put it in his backpack with Viele's map. "Let's go find my mom."

"It shouldn't be hard now," Euri said. "All we need to do is find those records."

She pulled Jack up so they were standing on the eagle's neck and then led him forward until they were wobbling in the wind on top of the eagle's head, seventy stories above the street. "Can you go slow?" he asked, trying to look anywhere but down.

With a glint in her eye, Euri squeezed his hand and jumped.

XV | Show Time

"Ahhhhh!" screamed Jack as they pitched headlong toward the street. He could hear the rush of the air as he fell, and above it, Euri's high-pitched cackles. A hundred feet from the ground she stopped short and hovered.

"I hate you," Jack said, as soon as he'd caught his breath.

"Come on! It was fun."

He glared at her.

"Oh, all right. I'll take it slower now, okay?"

As they chugged along at the same cautious speed as the old ghosts, he started to think about St. James. He was certain it was a church. It made sense that records for the dead would be kept in some crypt. "Are we far from St. James?"

"*The* St. James," she corrected.

As they flew down in big, lazy loops, Jack peered at the buildings on the busy street below. He expected to see a spire or church facade, but instead he saw oversize neon signs, cab wheels splashing through dirty banks of snow, and crushes of people gathering under brightly lit marquees. Running down the side of a large, not particularly churchlike building were the words ST. JAMES in white neon lights.

"It's not a church, is it?"

"A church?" Euri laughed. "Of course not. It's a theater."

They dropped soundlessly onto the sidewalk just as the last of the people who'd been waiting outside the St. James disappeared through its doors. THE PRODUCERS, read a smaller neon sign on the marquee—THE BEST SHOW EVER!

"I've wanted to see this ever since I died," Euri announced as they walked under the marquee and through a set of doors into a narrow hallway. "But it's impossible to get a ticket."

"Even if you're dead?"

They floated past two living ushers in red vests, up a flight of carpeted stairs, and then up a narrow, curving iron staircase. At the top of the stairs a third usher, a petite blond woman in a funny-looking red cap, stepped in front of him. "No ticket? Floating room only," she droned before handing them each a faded yellow playbill.

Jack began to pull it out of her hand when he felt some resistance. "Say, you look funny," she said, staring hard.

Euri quickly stepped between them. "He used to be one of the performers. Died with his makeup on, still looks kind of living, amazing what they can do with makeup now, huh?"

The usher grunted, and Jack felt her hand loosen on the program. "Enjoy the show," she said.

They floated through a door and onto a balcony that was nearly as high as the golden lyre embossed above the stage and that tilted at a precarious angle over it. Living people filled every seat—little old ladies loudly rifling through their bags for sucking candies; beefy tourists crammed into the narrow seats, laden with cameras and sightseeing guides; couples linked arm in arm, rosy after a few pre-theater drinks. Floating above their heads and in the cavernous expanse in front of them were hundreds of ghosts doing the same things. "How am I going to find Edna Gammon?" Jack asked. "She could be any one of these people."

Euri shrugged as they floated off the balcony, stopping under an enormous crystal chandelier. "Let's just watch some of the show and maybe we'll figure it out."

"But I don't have time. . . ." Jack started to say just as the theater lights dimmed and the orchestra started up. "Shhh!" said a plump old ghost floating behind them and wearing a silvery purple wig and a dead fox around her neck.

The orange curtain opened, revealing the outside of a

theater, and everyone burst into applause even though nothing had happened yet. Jack scanned his playbill. Above the black-and-white head shots of the actors was a warning printed in blocky letters:

Please do not howl, moan, groan, wail, sing along, rattle chains, or interfere in any way with the living performers in this show. Also please do not use flash.

Jack tapped Euri's shoulder. "I thought ghosts can't be heard by the living."

"Theaters are prone to paranormal interferences," she said. "If some ghost is really out of control, it can affect the show."

Onstage, a pair of ushers sprang out of the doors of the theater and began to sing about "opening night."

Euri was beaming. She seemed to have completely forgotten about the search for Jack's mom. Chorus members in ball gowns and tuxes filtered out of the wings onto the stage, belting out the rest of the song.

Jack yawned. But just when he was about to close his eyes, he noticed a woman wandering onstage dressed differently from the rest of the performers. Her short red hair was bobbed, and she wore a dressing gown. "'We're going to have a dandy little home!'" she began to warble, throwing her hands open to the audience.

Although she was making a racket, the living performers seemed oblivious to her presence. But all around him, ghosts began to grumble and shift. "Oh for God's sake," said the silvery-purple–haired old woman. "Do we have to hear *The Merry Malones* every night?"

"Edna, shut up!" shouted another.

Jack tugged on Euri's sleeve. "They said, 'Edna'! Do you think that's Edna Gammon?"

The silvery-purple–haired ghost leaned in between them. "You don't look like you've been dead long enough to remember Edna," she observed.

Jack noticed her giving him the familiar stare. "Well, I . . . I . . . wasn't. I just heard of her once."

"Once! You must know your theater. Most people haven't heard of her at all. She was the understudy for Polly Walker in *The Merry Malones*, back in 1927. Horrible musical. She died before she could take the stage."

"That may have been a good thing," Euri remarked as Edna fell to her knees screeching.

Suddenly, one of the living chorus girls tripped. "She's interfering with the performers!" someone shouted from near the ceiling.

A lightbulb hanging off a metal bar attached to the ceiling shattered, raining pieces of glass into the aisle. Living theatergoers jumped in their seats and scanned the ceiling. Jack half expected them to scream at the sight of hundreds of ghosts floating above, but they looked right through them. An usher ran down the aisle with a broom and dustpan. Someone onstage helped the chorus girl back to her feet, and the performers continued their song. Edna Gammon, her face as red as a newborn's, slumped to the floor. Then she leaped back to her feet and bowed. No one, either living or dead, applauded.

After several more bows, Edna skipped off into the darkness of the wings. "Come on," Jack said, pulling Euri down toward the stage. "Let's follow her."

"But the show's just started!"

"We came here to find my mom, remember?"

With an exaggerated sigh, Euri began to float down over the heads of the living audience and onto the stage. Up close, under the blazing lights, the performers were wearing garish amounts of blush and lipstick, even the men, and beads of sweat ran down their faces.

"This way," Jack said, pointing to the wings. They hovered a few inches above the stage floor, passing several stagehands holding props and techies in black T-shirts wearing headsets. They turned into an industrial-looking corridor lined with doors. "She probably went down here," Jack said.

Euri pointed to the brass nameplates stuck on the doors. "These are the stars' dressing rooms."

Jack pulled her along the rows of doors, but they all

seemed to be shut. "How are we going to find her? She could be in any of these."

Euri jerked to a halt. "Oh, you don't know how to think like a woman, do you? She's probably dying for visitors. Edna? Edna Gammon?" she trilled.

A door at the end of the corridor flew open, and Jack cringed, half expecting a living performer to come marching out to tell Euri to pipe down.

But instead a female voice cried out, "Fans for Edna Gammon?"

Before either of them had a chance to reply, Edna popped out of her dressing room and pretended to swoon against the door frame. "You shouldn't have," she said, coyly. "Flowers too?"

Jack looked at Euri in alarm. He hadn't brought any flowers.

But Edna just batted her eyes. "Darling, please don't say it was my best performance ever!"

"It . . . was . . . um . . ." Jack stuttered.

"Fabulous, darling?" she squealed. "You're too, too kind!"

Jack felt his cheeks turning red. "No, listen. I came to ask you about some records you keep. For ghosts who died eight years ago."

Euri elbowed him in the side, but it was too late. Edna's smile dropped off her face, her eyes narrowed, and she crossed her arms over her chest. "Talk to me in the morning," she hissed. "Records Division. Tunnel under Times Square. That's my day job."

She turned and slammed the door in their faces.

"At least she has one," Euri said. "Don't worry. We'll find out about your mom. Edna will be in a better mood in the morning."

"I was hoping to find my mom by then."

"Well, you clearly can't rush Edna. And in the meantime, you might as well see the rest of the city."

He and Euri spent the rest of the night "doing the tourist thing," as she called it. They visited the Guggenheim, a circular-shaped art museum of spiraling floors, where a ghost docent spoke with great reverence about the Calder mobiles; they strolled through the crowds of dead examining the long-life herbal supplements for sale in Chinatown; they took the elevator to the top of the Empire State Building (even though, as Euri pointed out, it would be much easier to fly). Just before dawn they followed an enticing beat down the escalator into the Times Square subway station and discovered a crew of ghosts drumming on plastic buckets. As if the musicians had cast a spell on him, Jack couldn't help but bob his head to the rhythm. He caught Euri watching him with a grin and stopped. But his foot began to tap instead. He looked at Euri with a helpless expression, and she started to laugh. Suddenly he began to laugh too. He jumped up and down and waved his arms. "That's it!" shouted one of the drummers.

Euri grabbed his hand and pulled him up into the air. They shimmied to the beat, trying silly moves—tap-dancing on the ceiling, moonwalking in midair. The drummers played faster and faster and, it seemed, just for them. Then, in a burst of percussion, the show ended, and the only sound in the station was the rattle of a subway train and the screech of its brakes. Still laughing, Jack and Euri returned to the park and joined the long line of ghosts, who whirled like a stream of water descending down the drain into the fountain.

XVI | Unnatural Things

As soon as they returned to the gray, stone passageways of the underground, Jack realized that all the dancing had made him tired. But another feeling overtook him as well: a deep, visceral sadness. The gloom affected him so much that he almost didn't want to find Edna, but instead rush back out of the underworld to the sunlight and his dad.

Euri spurred him on. "It's just mourning sickness," she explained. "We all feel it. Coming back in at dawn is a little like dying all over again. But this is your chance to find your mom! You may not find another golden bough again."

Jack nodded, but as he followed her through passageway after passageway, he was tempted to retrace his way back to the stairs and track 61. His father, by this time, would be frantic.

They reached a metal door with a lopsided plaque that said RECORDS DIVISION, and Euri knocked on it. "Yes?" said a familiar voice.

With a loud creak, the door opened, and Edna motioned

them inside. She looked completely different from the night before. Her red hair was tucked away in a hairnet, and though she was still wearing her dressing gown, a rusty metal pin was fastened to the lapel, which read, EDNA GAMMON, RECORDS DIVISION. PLEASED TO HELP YOU.

"What do you want?" she asked.

Jack smiled, but she stared back at him as if she'd never seen him before. Euri cut in. "We want to check the records for eight years ago. We're looking for an Anastasia . . . What's your mom's last name?" she asked, turning to Jack.

"Perdu," he said. "Anastasia Perdu."

Edna turned to a file cabinet covered in cobwebs, opened a drawer, and pulled out a thick, leather-bound book. "Perdu," she repeated, flipping through it. "Perdu. P—E—

"Here we go, the P-E's." She slammed the book onto her desk. Jack noticed that next to some ghosts' names was a stamp depicting an elegant bridge. "What's that mean?" he asked her.

"Moved on," said Edna flatly.

Jack gave Euri a worried look, but she squeezed his hand. "Don't worry. There's a good chance she's still here. And, look"—Euri pointed to a column titled *Favorite Haunts*—"as long as she's still here, it'll be easy for us to find her."

"'Peck,'" Edna droned, scanning the page with her finger.

Mrs. Peck had no bridge next to her name. Jack glanced at her favorite haunts: Bergdorf's shoe department and the Chanel counter at Bendel's.

"'Pellberg.'"

Mr. Pellberg haunted Katz's Deli and the chess tables in Washington Square Park. Or at least, he used to, because he had a bridge next to his name.

"'Pentaglio.'"

Mr. Pentaglio had no bridge and spent his nights at the Most Precious Blood Roman Catholic Church.

"'Pentokoglopolus.'"

"Now, there's a name," Euri said with admiration.

"There it is!" Jack cried, pointing over Edna's shoulder. "'Perdu, Anastasia.' That's her! And she has no bridge!" Then his fingers started to tingle as he realized something else. Unlike for everyone else on the page, there was nothing written in her *Favorite Haunts* column. The only mark was an asterisk. "What's that for?" he asked.

But before he could even point to it, Edna slammed the book shut and hastily stuffed it back into the file.

"Wait! Did you see that?" he asked Euri. "She had an asterisk. It must mean something."

He pulled at Edna's sleeve. "What does it mean?" When she turned back to him, he noticed her face was ashen. "Leave," she said to him, first softly then louder. "Leave! It's against the order of nature."

Even Euri looked taken aback. "What is?"

But Edna just gave them a shove out the door. "The office is closed!" she said. Then, for the second time in twenty-four hours, she slammed the door in their faces. The lights in her office switched off. A chain rattled across the door followed by the thump of a dead bolt.

"What are we going to do now?" Jack asked.

He looked at Euri. She was pacing back and forth. "'Against the order of nature,'" she mumbled under her breath. "People sometimes say that about . . ."

She started and looked up at Jack.

"What?"

The lightest tinge of red spread across her face. "Suicide."

"My mom didn't commit suicide!"

Euri remained quiet. The silence seemed like another accusation. "She didn't!" he repeated. "There was a high wind, and a scaffold fell on her!"

"I wasn't saying she did, okay!" Euri hissed. "I've seen . . . oh never mind. The asterisk must mean something else. Whatever it is, it doesn't happen much."

"Maybe my mom's not here. . . ."

"She didn't have a bridge," Euri interrupted. "So she hasn't moved on. That's one thing we know for sure."

"But maybe she's still alive?"

Euri shook her head. "Don't kid yourself. Why would she be in the ledger?"

Jack tried not to show his disappointment. "How are we going to find her now?"

"We'll find a way," she said. "Just give me a little time to think. She's got to be here somewhere."

He let Euri take his hand and lead him deeper into the tunnels. As he followed her, he wondered why she was so anxious to help him. But before he could ask, she said, "Tell me about the sun."

"The sun?"

"Yeah, remind me what it feels like. I haven't seen it in seven years."

Jack shrugged. "Warm, I guess."

"What else?"

Jack closed his eyes and tried to think. It was hard describing something so familiar. "At Yale, on sunny spring days, students study on blankets in the college courtyards. They take off their shoes."

"Just like people do in Central Park. And they put their bare feet in the grass," Euri said with a sigh.

A few minutes later, she directed Jack to a rickety cot in the corner of a small room. "It's time to rest. We're in an old electrical control room. No one will find you here."

"Are you going to sleep too?" Jack asked. He took off his backpack, leaned back on the cot, and stifled a yawn. Thinking about the sun had made him tired.

"The dead don't sleep. But I'll wake you in the evening. I think I know a place we can go where they know about unnatural things."

XVII | Occult Rites

Just before dusk, Euri woke Jack and led him through a crowded tunnel toward a different set of pipes. As he was funneled through them, Jack felt as if he'd been traveling through fountains his entire life—or death. The sensation of being squeezed through the pipes even felt good, like stretching out his muscles after a long sleep. Once again his fingers lost contact with Euri's, but just for a moment. Then her hand clasped around his and they shot into the sky beside a tower of white lights. As they slowed down, Jack realized that the tower of lights was an enormous Christmas tree, at least eighty feet tall, perched above a sunken terrace. He remembered his parents taking him here long ago. "Is this Rockefeller Center?" he asked.

Euri nodded and pointed down at a gold-leaf statue of a flying Prometheus frosted with snow, suspended over a backlit fountain. In front of it was a skating rink, where living skaters stumbled and spun, oblivious to the glowing spout of ghosts that emerged from the fountain behind them. "That's the Prometheus fountain," she said. "It's a popular scenic route when the tree is up."

Again, he felt the drop in his stomach as Euri jetted up into the sky. "We can't go too early," she said. "The type of ghosts we want to talk to won't be there till late at night. I can show you around more in the meantime."

As they flew over the city, Jack realized for the first time since he had arrived in New York that he had a sense of where he was. He recognized Fifth Avenue with its fancy shops and wide boulevard, then Grand Central Terminal with its statue of the Greek god Hermes, the messenger, on top. Just south of the terminal, he recognized another familiar building. "Hold it," he said to Euri. "That's where Dr. Lyons's office is." Jack explained about his visit to the doctor, how he had found his golden bough there, and the photo that the doctor had taken of him. "It was strange. That was pretty much the entire exam."

Euri listened attentively. "Did you ever see the photo?"

Jack shook his head. Euri dove straight toward one of the building's windows. "Well, let's take a look, then."

Instinctively, Jack closed his eyes as they passed through the glass and floated into an office where a man in a rumpled suit was shouting into a phone, "I said five hundred shares, not fifty!"

"I think it's a few floors up," Jack said.

They floated up into another office, where a weary-looking young woman sat typing at a desk. " 'The Numismatic Society of Greater New York devotes Volume MCCXII of our newsletter to the 1943 zinc-coated steel cent,' " she read aloud.

"Not this floor," said Jack.

They rose above the young woman's head and into a small office lined with leather-bound antique books and lit up by a dozen small candles. Jack squeezed Euri's hand. Dr. Lyons sat at his desk, his hands on a Ouija board indicator, and a stack of death certificates next to him. A red-haired ghost in a floor-length dress sat across from him, her hands also on the indicator. Dr. Lyons squinted down at one of the death certificates. "Are you Sally McGreevy?" he asked.

The ghost giggled and moved the indicator over the Ouija board to the letters **S-A-T-A-N**.

"Oh, please," said Euri. "That's the oldest trick in the book."

The red-haired ghost swung around and looked nervously at Jack and Euri. "You're not going to tell, are you? I'm just having some fun."

"Now, now," said Dr. Lyons. "We have to be honest with each other. I'm looking for a boy named Jack. Have you seen him?"

The red-haired ghost began to move the indicator toward the word **N-O** when Euri yanked her from the seat. "Hey, what are you doing?" the ghost shouted.

"Sorry," said Jack as Euri took her place. "But we have business here."

The red-haired ghost stomped her foot and then flew out the window. Euri slid the indicator toward the word **Y-E-S**.

Dr. Lyons leaned closer to the board. "Why should I believe you?"

"Tell him I took his subway token," Jack said.

"You can tell him yourself," Euri said. She stood up and gave Jack her seat.

He moved the indicator swiftly around the board. **T-O-O-K S-U-B-W-A-Y T-O-K-E-N**.

"That's true," said Dr. Lyons. "One of them is missing."

W-H-E-R-E J-A-C-K-S P-H-O-T-O, Jack spelled.

"Who are you?" Dr. Lyons asked. "And is Jack okay?"

YES T-E-L-L H-I-S D-A-D W-H-E-R-E P-H-O-T-O.

Dr. Lyons opened up the drawer and took out the photo. He placed it on the Ouija board. Euri laughed. "Either you're not very photogenic or that camera is lousy."

Jack peered down at himself. His hair was white, his body translucent—he was completely overexposed. But then he noticed something strange. "Look," he said, pointing to the desk and couch in the background. "I'm the only thing that's overexposed. Everything else looks normal."

Euri stopped smiling. "That's weird."

Jack turned back to the Ouija board. **W-H-A-T-S W-R-O-N-G**, he spelled. But before he could finish, the red-haired ghost blew back through the window. "They're over here," she cried. "Just like I found them. Talking with the living!" The candles in the room blew out as an enormous guard tumbled through the window.

"Come on!" said Euri. Jack knocked the indicator off the board as she yanked him through the floor and into the Numismatic Society office. Then she pulled him through the window, and they flew away at top speed.

"That tattletale," said Euri, once they were a safe distance away from Dr. Lyons's building. "If I ever see her again . . ."

But Jack wasn't thinking about the red-haired ghost. "Are you sure I'm not dead?" he asked. "The photo . . ."

"If you were dead how could you have had a whole conversation with Dr. Lyons after you arrived in New York?" Euri interrupted. "He saw you, right?"

"Yes, but he's clearly no ordinary doctor. . . ."

"He's a doctor of the paranormal," Euri interrupted. "He can communicate with the dead through the occult, but he obviously doesn't see them. So if he saw you before, you're alive. And you went to Grand Central afterward and other living people saw you, right?"

Jack thought about the woman who asked him if he wanted to listen at the whispering gallery, and nodded.

"Then you're not dead," Euri concluded. "Forget about the photo. Probably something was just wrong with the camera. I'll show you more of the city till it's late enough to find the sort of ghosts who might know about that asterisk."

They flew across town and through the walls of a round coliseum-like building. "Madison Square Garden," Euri announced as they emerged into a brightly lit stadium. Men in white jerseys and green jerseys ran up and down a shiny basketball court, their rubber sneakers squeaking on the wood as they shifted direction with the referee's whistle. On ascending tiers of bleachers sat hundreds of living fans, and above their heads, as high up as the JumboTron, floated hundreds more dead ones. Jack didn't watch a lot of basketball but he recognized the players in white. "Those are the Knicks?"

Euri nodded. "And those are the former Knicks," she said, pointing to several tall ghosts in kneesocks and outdated jerseys who flew swiftly alongside the hometown players, clamoring for the ball. "Come on, let's get a seat."

Jack expected her to float up above the living fans, but instead she whizzed over the players' heads and perched atop one of the backboards. Jack looked around, but before he could figure out whether anyone minded them being there, a stampede of players rushed toward them, and a tangle of arms shot into the air. Then the ball whooshed through the net and the backboard trembled. The living and dead fans began to roar as the whole stadium shook. Jack shouted along with the rest of the crowd. "This is amazing!" he said to Euri as the roar died down and the players raced to the other end of the court.

Euri smiled, looking pleased. "Best seats in the house."

After the Knicks game was over, as on the previous night, Euri kept them on an exhausting itinerary: the Apollo theater in Harlem, where they listened to the living and the dead's comedy routines; FAO Schwarz, where they raced around the darkened store in miniconvertibles until Jack crashed into a giant stuffed zebra; Tiffany's, where they floated through the locked vault of an entrance, and even Jack was impressed by the world's largest diamond.

Finally, in the early morning hours, they sped west toward Seventh Avenue. Times Square burst into technicolor bloom, then in a flash it was gone. The buildings began to get smaller, the streets darker. Little restaurants and bars glowed warmly below. At the green-and-white sign for Commerce Street they began to descend. It was quieter here. Only a few people were out, shivering as they walked their dogs or hurried home from a night on the town. Steam billowed up from a manhole. Euri turned onto a small street. No one, living or dead, was on it.

"Damn," Euri said, yanking Jack back the way they'd come. "This is the hardest place to find."

After a few steps she stopped. "There it is," she said, pointing to a small, arched door.

"There what is?" Jack asked. The door didn't even have a sign, just the number 86.

"Chumley's," said Euri, pulling him through the door.

XVIII | Chumley's

Jack went up four steps, then down four steps, turned a corner, and found himself standing in a series of dimly lit rooms. Sawdust covered the wood floors, and two old Labrador retrievers stretched out in front of the dying embers of the fireplace, whining in their sleep. The walls were covered with a combination of photos of New York City firefighters and famous authors, as well as some of their book jackets. Two dozen ghosts dressed in old-fashioned clothes, all with the same wan faces and flat, lifeless eyes, floated beside the wooden tables. A ghost bartender washed glasses by the bar. "Where are the living?" Jack asked.

"The place closed hours ago," said Euri. Lowering her voice, she added, "But I'm sure someone here will be able to tell us more. Chumley's used to be a speakeasy during Prohibition. That's why the door is so hard to find. You can see it's just a regular old bar now, but there are still some weird old ghosts that hang out here." She pointed to a table at the back of the bar. "See that guy?"

A stubbly gray face hung in the shadowy corner like a gargoyle. The ghost sat alone, one thick hand mechanically reaching down for a glass and lifting it to his lips. "I bet he's been coming here a long time," Euri continued. "He may know something about that asterisk."

They weaved through the crowd, but as they came closer to the man's table, Jack noticed that the grizzled ghost wasn't by himself. Sitting next to him in the shadows was a flapper who looked a few years older than Jack and Euri. She wore a beaded green dress that ended midthigh, and a feather in her hair. Her bobbed black hair framed a pair of dark, catlike eyes. They flashed up at Euri and Jack. "Well, lookie here, Harry. We have visitors."

The ghost with the massive, stone face nodded but said nothing.

"You look underage," the flapper said, pointing at Jack. "Not that I care," she added with a yawn.

"Well, you look underage yourself," Euri shot back.

The ghost in the green dress looked Euri up and down. "Not so good dying in a school uniform, is it, sister?"

Jack could see a small vein on Euri's temple throb. She looked ready to say something really nasty. He decided to step in. "We want to talk to him," he said, pointing to the stone-faced man. "We need some information."

"Him?" said the ghost in the green dress. "What does he know?"

"Well," Jack stammered. "We need someone who's been dead awhile. Who might know about some of the . . . the unnatural things that can happen."

A hoarse, croaky voice cut in. "I been dead only seventeen years," said the old-looking ghost.

Jack looked at Euri, who had crossed her arms and was working her jaw in an angry way. He raised his eyebrows to signal that maybe they should go.

"What 'unnatural' things?" asked the ghost in the green dress, narrowing her eyes.

Jack didn't answer.

"Sit down," she said, patting the space next to her. "Level with me, and maybe I can help you. Bartender!"

Jack looked uncertainly at Euri, but she was fingering the skirt of her uniform. A busty barmaid blew through the wall. "Yeah?"

"Four spirits."

The barmaid didn't move. "How old are you?"

"For crying out loud, Trixie," said the ghost in the green dress. "I'm ninety-seven. Old enough to have a drink."

Turning to Jack, she explained, "I died eighty years ago. I'm ancient."

"Well how's about those two?" the barmaid said, pointing to him and Euri.

"I'm twenty-one!" Euri said smugly, forgetting her skirt. "I died seven years ago."

Everyone turned to Jack. "Uh, me too," he said.

"He doesn't look that dead to me," droned the barmaid before she disappeared back through the wall.

A minute later the drinks arrived: three tumblers and a glass of soda with a straw. Jack tried to hide his disappointment when the waitress slammed the soda down in front of him. "Don't drink it," whispered Euri. Jack remembered the *Unofficial Guide* and fiddled with the straw instead.

"To death," said the cat-eyed ghost, holding up her glass.

"To death," said her grizzled companion, knocking back his drink and emitting a satisfied burp.

Euri mumbled something indecipherable and took a small swallow of her drink.

"To death," said Jack. He winked at Euri then held up his drink and stuck the straw between his lips, pretending to take a sip.

After a while the ghost in the green dress spoke. "I'm Ruby," she said. "This here is Harry. I was stabbed to death, so I don't like knives. Harry froze on the street."

"Was a night like this," he added. "I was drunk."

Ruby turned to Jack. "How'd you die?"

"Train."

"A tragic bunch. How about you?" she asked, cocking her head toward Euri.

Jack waited to hear what Euri would say. "Accident," she said after a pause.

Ruby chuckled. "Is death ever not? Care to specify?"

Euri shifted in her seat. "Not really."

"Okay, Miss Mysterious." She looked back at Jack, studying his eyes. "You're a funny lot, you two. What do you want, anyhow?"

"We want to know about an asterisk," Jack explained.

"What asterisk?"

"We went to look someone up in the death records and she had an asterisk next to her name. The record keeper seemed upset by it. Do you know what it means?"

Ruby shrugged. "An asterisk? I have no idea. A cross, I know. A circle . . ." She turned to Euri. "You're all secretive. I bet you have a circle."

"What's a circle?" asked Jack.

"Shut up," Euri hissed at Ruby. "It was an accident."

Jack felt confused. "So you don't know anything about an asterisk?"

Ruby shrugged. "Can't help you, kid."

"It was an accident," Euri repeated. She looked like she wanted to cry.

"You got anything else to go on?" Ruby asked.

Jack opened his backpack and pulled out the map. "This."

Ruby grabbed the map out of his hands and studied it. "Hey, isn't this the map that fellow used years ago?" she said, sliding it across the table to Harry.

Harry pulled the map closer to his stubbly face.

"What fellow?" asked Jack.

"The one who broke in. The living one," Ruby said.

"Yeah," mumbled Harry. "It is."

XIX | Trapped

For a second Jack thought that they were talking about him. But then he remembered that Ruby had said that the man had come in years ago. "Tell me more," he begged.

Even Euri had stopped brooding over the circle business. "Yeah, what happened?" she asked.

Ruby bent forward and whispered, "A living fellow came into the underworld. He wanted to take away some woman. Said they were in love."

Jack stared at his mother's name written in the corner of the map. Had his father come to the underworld like Orpheus, and tried to bring his mother back? Is that why she had an asterisk next to her name? "Was he a professor? A big man with a beard?"

Harry cut in. "We never saw him. But I thought he was some sort of teacher or something."

Euri grabbed Harry's arm. "What happened to her?" she asked. "Did it work?"

"He went back up. I'm not sure what happened to her."

Jack had a powerful feeling that the man had been his father, but there was one way to find out for sure. "Was it eight years ago? Was that when he came?"

Harry nodded.

Jack squeezed Euri's hand under the table.

But a voice interjected. "No, it was definitely further back than that." They both turned to Ruby.

"What do you mean?" Jack said. "It had to be eight years ago!"

She shook her head. "It happened sixteen years ago."

Harry cocked his head and made calculations on his hands. "She's probably right," he finally said. "I got a bad head for dates."

"Are you sure?" Jack asked. His mother had been alive sixteen years ago, so there would have been no reason for his father to go to the underworld to find her. The man must have been someone else. He couldn't believe he was wrong. He folded up the map and put it in his pocket.

"It was definitely sixteen years ago," repeated Ruby. "It happened the same year that the fellow who murdered me finally died." Her eyebrows arched slightly and her black eyes flickered at Jack. "You know there's something funny about you. It's almost like you're alive. . . ."

"He just died," Euri interjected. "He's new."

But Ruby ignored her. "If I didn't know better, I might think you followed that map down here yourself. It's funny he has the map, isn't it, Harry?" She gave a laugh that made the hair on the back of Jack's neck prickle.

Suddenly, the two old labs in front of the fireplace staggered to their feet and began to bark and then whine. "Quiet!" shouted the bartender. The horse-size three-headed dog barreled into the bar in a tracking posture, dragging one of the thick-necked guards after him, and sniffed at a short, heavyset ghost, who dropped his drink in terror.

"Stay calm. We'll just go through the wall," Euri whispered. She turned to Ruby and Harry. "So long, we've got to run."

Standing next to Cerberus and his handler was the uniformed guard from the photograph, with the bushy mustache and nightstick. "Stay where you are," he shouted in the cold, commanding voice that Jack remembered from when he was wedged into the tunnel. "We have the walls surrounded."

"What are we going to do now?" Jack whispered to Euri.

Euri looked frantically around the bar. "I don't know."

"Jeepers, creepers, it's Clubber Williams," said Ruby.

Jack remembered Professor Schmitt's warning. "Who exactly *is* Clubber Williams?"

Ruby looked at Jack as if he were crazy. "Who's Clubber Williams? He was only the most corrupt cop in the city's history. He averaged a fight a day in Hell's Kitchen, then made hundreds of thousands of dollars terrorizing the Tenderloin." She pointed to his nightstick. "You can guess how he got his name."

Jack stared at the shiny, black nightstick as Clubber joined the other guard, who led Cerberus, sniffing and growling, toward the middle of the bar. Another ghost in a flapper outfit stood with her arms in the air, quivering as Cerberus sniffed her ankles. "I'm really dead!" she repeated over and over again.

"There's got to be a reason why Clubber's here," said Ruby as she stared at Jack. Slowly her glance fell on his soda. "Why aren't you drinking that?"

Jack tried to give a casual-looking shrug. "I'm not thirsty."

Ruby picked up the glass and held it to his lips. "Well, why don't you just take a little sip for us. . . ."

Euri knocked the glass out of Ruby's hands.

"Jumping Jehovahs, Harry," said Ruby. "I knew it! He's alive!"

Jack looked helplessly at Euri.

"It's not what you think," Euri said to Ruby.

But Ruby just grinned at her. "The jig is up, sister."

The other flapper ghost moaned in terror. "It's not

her," said Clubber as Cerberus followed the trail deeper into the bar.

Ruby chuckled. "Boy, have you got yourself in a jam. You almost had me fooled, though. You look pretty dead for someone who's still kicking."

"They're heading this way!" Jack whispered. "I'm going to die."

Ruby shrugged and took a sip of her drink. "What's wrong with that?"

Euri grabbed a steak knife and lunged across the table, brandishing it at Ruby. "A lot's wrong with that! You've got to help him."

For the first time that evening, the mirth behind Ruby's eyes faded. "Easy, sister," she mumbled. "I was just razzing you."

Euri pointed the knife in the direction of Cerberus, Clubber, and the other guard, who were all moving toward them through the crowd. "Don't worry, Jack," she said. "They'll have to get through me first."

Jack looked at the steak knife shaking in her hands and grabbed his own knife. "They'll have to get through both of us."

"Touching," said Ruby. "But this is a juice joint. There's always more than one way out."

"Where?" asked Jack and Euri simultaneously.

"Well, there's the bookcase," she said. "It's really a

secret door that leads to an alley. But it's right by the entrance. There's no way you can make it that far without being noticed. And anyway, Clubber said they've got the walls surrounded."

"Maybe we can fly up through the ceiling?" Jack suggested.

"They'll notice anyone who flies up," said Ruby. "But they may not notice someone who disappears down." She pointed to a door in the floor near the bar. "There's a small cellar beneath the bar where they used to hide spirits during Prohibition. Clubber died before Prohibition so I doubt he knows about it. If you descend through the trapdoor, you should be smack dab in the center of it, and you can float into the basements of neighboring houses."

"Thank you!" said Jack, scrambling to his feet.

"Wait, Jack," whispered Euri, pulling him back down. "The guards are practically there already."

Cerberus sniffed the ground near the bar and howled. "He's got the scent back!" said the thick-necked guard.

"It's about time," Clubber snarled.

"We'll create a diversion," said Harry. "Ruby's always good at that."

"Jeez, Harry, I was just getting comfortable," said Ruby, but she stood up and put her hand on Euri's shoulder. Jack heard her whisper, "Tell the kid about your circle, sister. It's nothing to be ashamed of. He'll understand."

Jack noticed Euri wince as Ruby squeezed her hand.

Then Ruby and Harry flew toward the bar, and Ruby ground the heel of her shoe into one of Cerberus's bear-size paws. All three of his heads squealed as he leaped backward, momentarily stunned. Clubber and the guard seized Ruby while Cerberus gnashed and bared three heads' worth of teeth at her, preparing to attack.

"She's going to die!" Jack said.

"Too late for that," said Euri.

But Ruby struggled, floating her legs, which kicked wildly in the air. As the crowd of Chumley's ghosts watched in alarm, she shouted, "Dead eighty years and I need that mutt down my throat? What's the matter with you? Let me go!"

Harry tackled the thick-necked guard and knocked him back into the first room of the bar, away from the cellar. "That's right. Let her go!" he shouted as they rolled across the sawdust-covered floor, the living labs barking and scampering after them as other ghosts tried to break them up. Clubber dragged Ruby after them, Cerberus snapping at her still-kicking heels.

"Come on," whispered Euri. She grabbed Jack's hand and they ran to the trapdoor. Jack watched his feet disappear through the floor, then his knees and waist and chest. But just before his head disappeared, he saw Cerberus suddenly swing around and scramble toward them, barking.

Jack closed his eyes, and when he next opened them, they were in a dark, cramped cellar with a sour-smelling, sticky floor. Aluminum kegs were lined up against the wall and attached to rubber hoses that led up to the bar through holes bored into the ceiling, and cardboard cases filled with glass bottles were stacked across the floor. Euri held her finger to her lips. Overhead, he could hear Ruby shouting over Cerberus's loud barking. Euri flew to the cellar wall and pulled Jack through it and into the basement of the house next door. It was a dingy room with a washing machine and dryer and some old bikes. The floorboards creaked above them, and they could still hear faint shouting from Chumley's. "The guards may be upstairs," Euri mouthed.

She pointed to another wall, and Jack nodded as she once again pulled him through it and into a darkened basement room, where a couple slept huddled together on a pullout sofa. He and Euri hovered in the gloom, listening for any noises, but this building was quiet. Euri looked at the couple. Their quilt had fallen off the bed, and she lifted it from the floor and gently draped it back over them. Jack realized he looked surprised, because she shrugged and said, "Sometimes I remember feeling cold."

Her expression turned stern. "Let's go." Tightening her grip around Jack's hand, she flew up through the ceiling, into a kitchen, and through the window. Outside, the sky was still dark, but more lights began to twinkle on in apartments, and a few trucks delivering newspapers or milk to the grocers rumbled down the street. "We don't want to go to a fountain too close by, in case the guards have it staked out," Euri explained. "Columbus Circle is probably safest."

As they flew up Eighth Avenue, Jack looked at the homeless wrapped in cardboard and blankets sleeping on the sidewalk; and the coffee vendors arranging Danishes and bagels in their carts. Every few blocks, the street echoed with the thunderous roll of a metal security door being lifted, and the living began to emerge in greater number from their apartments, sleepy and balancing cups of coffee, into the predawn darkness. Just as the first cold pink light rose over the city, Euri landed in front of a granite column. From the base of it jutted the stone bow of a boat with an angel on top and a fountain beneath it.

"I have something to tell you," Euri whispered as they joined the last few ghosts disappearing into the mouths of the stone fish at the bottom of the fountain.

"What?"

"Not now," she said. "When we get back under."

XX | Euri's Secret

As Euri led him through a series of tunnels toward the outer edges of the underworld, Jack fingered the map in his pocket. He'd felt certain that the living man who'd come here before had been his father. But the dates made it impossible.

He followed Euri into a small, brick room with an arched roof that reminded him of a wine cellar. "Where are we?" he asked.

Euri pointed to a lone chair and gestured for him to sit. "In a room under one of the pillars of the Brooklyn Bridge."

Jack looked up and tried to imagine the bridge soaring above him, cars packed on it in their morning commute. But inside the bridge, it was quiet and dark. He took off his backpack and stifled a yawn. "Did you want to tell me something?"

Euri froze. "Maybe you're tired. You should sleep."

"I don't want to sleep. I only have one more night left. Is it about the circle?"

"Yes," Euri said.

She paused, and Jack waited for her to continue. "The circle means suicide. I have a circle."

He tried to look as understanding as possible, knowing she was watching for his reaction. "I'm sorry," he said.

"It's no big deal. Except for the fact that I'm dead."

"How did you . . . ?" he asked awkwardly.

"I was hit by a train," Euri said. "I know, familiar story, right?"

"Why?"

Euri shrugged. "Because I jumped in front of it."

Jack shook his head. "No, I mean, why did you do it?"

"Listen, I've told you about the circle," she snapped. "That's all you need to know. It was my own stupid fault."

She floated over to a corner of the room and pretended to inspect some bricks poking out of the wall. Jack heard a soft sniffle, and before he could stop himself, he stood up. "Euri."

"What?" she said without turning around.

He wanted to tell her how no one had ever shared such a deep secret with him before—and how it made him feel, for the first time, like he truly had a friend. But this was too hard to explain. "There's this Latin word in the *Metamorphoses*: *occidere*. It could mean 'to be killed' or 'to perish' . . ." And then suddenly Jack remembered another meaning of *occidere* that he hadn't considered before. "Or," he quietly added, "'to die by one's own hand.'" He searched for the right words. "But my interpretation is 'to perish.' Whatever happened, I don't think it was your fault. It was an accident."

She turned to him and nodded gratefully. "I want to go back."

Jack didn't know what to say. There was no way back for her.

A tiny voice emerged from the corner of the room. "Euri, are you sad again?"

Jack started. A small, towheaded child in a smocked dress hovered midair. "It's not so bad here," said the tiny ghost.

A dozen small children blew through the door and into the room like dandelion seeds. "Euri," they called, echoing each other. "Don't be sad."

Euri waved them away, but Jack noticed that the corners of her mouth were fighting a smile. She floated back over next to Jack. The children drifted down around them and settled on the floor. They were elementary-school age, and several wore torn and tattered outfits. "Tonight we're going to the play!" cried a boy in thick glasses and pajamas.

"Really, Wilson? The play?" Euri repeated. "That's nice."

The girl in the smocked dress pointed to Jack. "Who's he?"

"This is Jack," said Euri. Jack made an awkward wave.

"I'm Mary," she said with a curtsy.

"Mary is older than everyone else," said Wilson. "And especially me because I died last year."

"I'm two hundred and thirteen," said Mary. "How old are you?"

"Fourteen," said Jack.

The children laughed. "Are you still alive?" said a skinny boy in a long, dirty nightshirt.

Even though they were just little kids, Jack felt annoyed. "No. I just died recently."

"He looks alive!" declared the boy.

"Eli, you're being rude," said Wilson to the boy. He adjusted his glasses and turned to look at Jack. "It's okay. Some of the older ghosts think I look alive too. Are you going to come with us to the play?"

Euri shook her head. "I don't think so," said Jack.

A very tiny girl pulled on Jack's pant leg and pointed to the ceiling. "But it's about a man who came from up there."

"From up where?" Jack asked.

"From the living world," Mary interrupted. "Here, look. You can see the flyer."

She handed Jack a thin paper announcement. TONIGHT, AT 2 A.M., THE PLAY-IN-THE-PARK SERIES PRESENTS THE UNDERWORLD PREMIERE OF *THE BRIDE'S PLAY*, BY TENNESSEE WILLIAMS.

Beneath a black-and-white photo of a man clutching a woman in a passionate embrace, Jack read, "'Based on true events, *The Bride's Play* is a haunting new twist on Ovid's classic tale of love between the living and the dead.'"

Jack looked at Euri. "Based on true events?" he repeated.

Euri shook her head. "Don't get your hopes up, Jack. They have these plays every week. Gives the dead playwrights something to do. It's not really true."

"Yes it is!" shouted the littlest ghost.

For a moment Euri looked surprised. Then she pulled the tiny girl onto her lap and gave her a kiss. "Of course it is, Annie," she said.

"Will you come with us, Euri?" asked Wilson. "You never come."

"It's just another story about how the dead can't go back; just the living," she said wearily. "I don't think so."

"Oh, please!" begged Mary.

"Come on, Euri," Jack said. "We're out of clues."

The child ghosts began to chant. "Please, Euri, come!"

Euri looked over her little crew. Then her eyes found Jack's. "Okay, okay. Jack and I will come tonight, but we have to talk about grown-up things first. So go off, and we'll meet you at your playground at one a.m. before the performance."

A cheer rose up from the band of child ghosts as they floated into the air and tumbled through the door and back out to the maze of tunnels. "They're just children," Jack remarked after they had left. "It doesn't seem fair. Why don't they move on?"

"Because children have problems too," said Euri, "and sometimes the younger they are, the bigger they feel."

"I only have one more night," said Jack, remembering his own.

"I know," said Euri. "But let's not think about that now. We'll figure out something. In the meantime, you're still alive. You need to get some sleep."

Jack obediently lay down, balled up his jacket, and put it under his head. Euri floated above him. Jack closed his eyes then opened them. "Euri?"

"What?"

Euri had told him her secret—he could tell her his fear. "How could I have been destined to come here and not find my mom?"

For a moment Euri was silent. "Maybe that's not who you were destined to find."

"Maybe," he said.

"Never mind. I'm sure it is. We'll find her tomorrow. Now get some rest."

"I'm not really tired," he protested. But the word "tired" was interrupted by a yawn, and as soon as he closed his eyes he fell into a dreamless sleep.

XXI | Pilgrim Hill

Just after sunset, Jack spiraled up through Bethesda fountain, his hand briefly losing contact with Euri's as he shot
out of the fountain and up over the park. As her fingers
settled back around his, he realized this was probably the
last night he would ever fountain-travel. He gripped Euri's
hand tighter and tried to take everything in. A yellow-
tinged full moon drifted through the clouds, and there
was electricity in the air that made the whole city seem
expectant. Euri nervously scanned the snow-covered park
for Clubber and the guards, but they seemed to be in
another part of the underworld, hunting other souls. Only
a lone, faint howl echoed across the park.

"So where are we going tonight?" Jack asked, trying to
be upbeat.

"To haunt."

Jack smiled playfully at her. "I thought you didn't
haunt."

But Euri didn't smile back. She began to fly swiftly

across the park to Fifth Avenue. Soon, Jack recognized the apartment building with the stone cornucopia and garlands that they had haunted his first night in the underworld. Euri flew up to the penthouse and pulled him onto the living room window ledge. Through the window, Jack could see the familiar family tableau—the parents and the little girl sitting on the floor this time, playing a game by the fire. "They never go out," Euri said through gritted teeth.

Jack pulled gently on her arm. "Euri, why are we here?"

Like his mother in the park, her eyes glazed over and she didn't answer him. But Jack wasn't going to give up. "Are they your parents?"

Euri turned around and looked at him solemnly. "No. My parents were nothing like them."

Jack looked at her skeptically, but she didn't blink. "What were your parents like?"

"They"—Euri thought for a moment—"didn't notice me. They weren't ever around. They hardly cared when I died."

"I'm sure that's not true."

"They forgot about me."

"That would be impossible," Jack said.

For the first time that evening, Euri smiled, but there were tears in her eyes. "I don't want you to go," she said.

Jack put his arm around her. "You know what? Why

are we standing out here?" He pointed through the window at the glittering tree and the inviting living room. "That's ours too."

"It's not . . ."

"Take us in," Jack insisted.

Euri reluctantly pulled him in through the window, and Jack ran over to the couch and threw himself on it. "Come on, Euri! Tonight it's ours."

Euri hesitated.

"Forget them," Jack said, waving off the family.

Euri floated over and sat primly next to him.

"You won, Janie. It's time for bed," the man said.

"No, not yet!" the little girl cried.

Euri began to pick at her skirt.

"Relax," said Jack. "Pretend you're alive."

"It's going to snow more tonight," the woman said, "and tomorrow I'll take you sledding in the park."

Jack pictured his mom saying the same thing. For a moment he felt as glum as Euri. There was almost no chance he would find her. But then he realized that he had found someone else. "Look, they're going to bed," he said as the man carried Janie out of the room and the woman followed. Euri gradually leaned against him. The fire crackled. As the clock ticked heavily in the silent room, Jack put his arm around her, wishing he could protect her from ever feeling unhappy or alone.

"Perhaps there's something for us under the tree?" he said.

Euri rolled her eyes. "Oh, sure."

He stood up and surveyed the toys and stuffed animals. Everything had already been unwrapped. His gaze wandered up the enormous tree, laden with elaborate silver-and-glass ornaments that reflected the white lights. He suddenly noticed one ornament resting near the top that was different from the rest—a faded construction paper angel with macaroni hair and a red-crayon smile. DEIRDRE was scrawled across the angel's dress in a child's tilted block letters.

"Did you find anything?" Euri asked.

"Yes," said Jack. He picked up a stuffed bear and handed it to her.

"It's not wrapped."

"The wrapping paper is ghostly. You just can't see it. There's a big bow too."

"Jack!" Euri said, pelting him with the bear.

Jack knew his joke was stupid, but for some reason they both started laughing so hard that he half expected the living couple to march in and tell them to be quiet.

"Come on," Euri finally said. "It's your last night. Let's get out of here." She grabbed his hand. "Where do you want to go?"

Jack hesitated. "Can we do anything?"

"Anything."

"Let's go sledding."

"That," said Euri, "is a ridiculous idea. I know just the place."

Minutes later, they were standing on top of a sloped knoll in Central Park. Jack looked around. Behind them was a statue of a pilgrim leaning on his rifle and looking out over taxis rushing across the park at Seventy-second Street. Over the tree line on Fifth Avenue, Jack could see apartment buildings jutting up into the sky. At the bottom of the hill was a walking path, and beyond that, a large man-made oval pond. "I remember this place."

"It's Pilgrim Hill. Everyone in New York goes sledding here."

Jack peered down the hill. A few living people hurried along the path, but no one living or dead was sledding. Euri craned her neck at something leaning against a tree near the bottom of the hill and took off in the air.

"Where are you going?" Jack called after her.

She didn't answer, but as she swooped back up the hill, Jack could see she was carrying a large, orange plastic object in her hands. "Luckily, one of the living left a sled," she said when she reached him, dropping it onto the snow. "You're in back," she directed. "Put your arms around my waist."

As Jack climbed in behind her, he could feel his heart

beating with anticipation, just like when he had gone sledding with his mom. "Give a push," Euri ordered.

Jack pushed off against the snowy ground and they scooted forward past bulbous tree trunks. The sled began to slide down the hill, and as they gained momentum it bounced over the snow. Jack clutched Euri and grinned up at the night sky, watching the spindly tree branches and the clouds blur overhead.

"Here comes a big bump!" shouted Euri. "Hold on! Hold on!"

They hit a pile of snow and flew into the air. Jack braced himself for the shock of landing, but they kept flying higher and higher. Euri shrieked as they sailed over the walking path at the bottom of the hill. Then the bottom of the sled scraped against tree branches, and Jack realized that they were flying over trees and the roof of a small brick kiosk, toward the frozen pond. Jack felt his stomach flip as they began to plummet back to earth. With a shout, he closed his eyes.

The sled landed with a thump and began sliding quickly. Euri was laughing, and Jack opened his eyes just as they skidded to a stop. They were at the far end of the frozen pond in front of a snow-coated statue of Alice sitting on a toadstool, surrounded by the Mad Hatter, the Cheshire Cat, and the White Rabbit.

Euri turned around to look at him. "I probably should

have told you that sledding is a little different when you can fly. Are you all right?"

For a moment Jack didn't speak. Then, over his own racing breath, he found his voice. "Again," he said. "Let's do it again."

XXII | The Bride's Play

Several hours later, Jack still didn't want to stop. On one run they had hit the bump so hard that they'd sledded all the way from Pilgrim Hill to the Harlem Meer thirty blocks north. But as the clouds thickened, Euri abandoned the sled where they had found it and they flew toward the shrieks and laughter that emanated from children on the other side of Seventy-second Street. They flew over an iron gate and into a playground bathed by the soft glow of the streetlights on Fifth Avenue. The pale forms of children dashed around them, scrambling up a rope spiderweb and pumping their legs through the air on tire swings.

Wilson was the first to spot them. "Euri! Jack!" he shouted as he flew down from a colorfully painted jungle gym. The rest of the child ghosts floated in a circle around them. "You're here!" they cried. "You're here!"

Euri looked pleased with her reception. "Well, we said we'd be."

"We didn't believe you," said Wilson. He turned to

Jack. "Euri mostly stays alone under the bridge. She goes out only by herself—"

"Wilson," Euri interrupted. "I'm here now. Let's go."

They rose into the sky like a flock of birds, he and Euri at the front, the child ghosts behind them. As he flew, Jack decided that except for Cerberus, death really wasn't as bad as Euri made it seem. At night the whole city was yours, and you could just kick up your heels and fly as high as you wanted above the skyscrapers and the city lights.

Jack looked down and caught his breath. On a giant, moonlit meadow in the middle of the park, thousands of ghosts were lounging on the snow. A living German shepherd raced around the field, barking as a child landed in the snow in front of it; then the dog looked up at the sky and darted off to chase another.

"Finn! Finnegan! What are you doing? There's nothing there," his owner shouted from the meadow's edge.

Euri floated down to the ground, and, as the child ghosts flew over to the special section of the meadow reserved just for them, she pulled Jack behind her, squeezing her way up to the front of the crowd. They sat down in the snow next to a ghost with wire-framed glasses and jutting ears who was furiously scribbling in a notebook. Jack couldn't help peeking over his shoulder.

"It's a review," the man said imperiously, without looking up.

"Oh," said Jack, embarrassed that he'd been caught snooping.

"When Tennessee died in the Hotel Elysee in 1983, the majority of his talent died with him," the man continued. "This promises to be god-awful. Far worse than *Orpheus Descending*."

"Orpheus . . . ?"

The man gave him an impatient glance. "The last time Tennessee tried to retell the Orpheus myth, in 1957. I quote my own review, 'But it seems to this playgoer that Mr. Williams has his story less thoroughly under control this time, and his allusive style has a less sturdy foundation.'"

Jack wasn't sure how to respond, so he turned his attention to the stage. It was large and igloo-like, fashioned entirely from snow. A gossamer curtain made of frost hung down over it.

Suddenly, the curtain rustled and a man with a mustache and dressed in a white suit floated through it. "All hail, Tennessee," said the critic wearily. The crowd murmured with excitement and then grew silent until the only sound was the sweep of the wind across the field. The man opened his arms and began to speak in a Southern accent:

"Alone we are on this great earth,
Lonesome spirits from our birth.
Which is why when love prevails
We'll gladly brave the darkest trails.
For example, you may have read
How Orpheus came down to the dead,
Searching for the bride he lost
Because he knew what true love cost.
But the living can't see the side
Of the underworld bride,
Who chose to sacrifice her death,
Who traded eternity for breath.
This is her story, based on fact,
Which our humble players will reenact.
Remember spirits, with those above,
To not look back if you choose love."

"The purple patches of poetry leave this critic cold," declared the critic, jotting down his own words as the playwright bowed. "Tennessee should stick to prose."

Jack shrugged. "I thought it was okay."

The critic sighed. "That, young man, is why the world needs critics."

As the playwright floated backstage, the curtain of frost vanished, melting away in tiny bursts of silver light. Behind it, fashioned from snow, was a room covered with what looked to be scrolls of paper. A group of men pored over one of them. "The original springs and rivers of Manhattan," said the tallest of the group. "If we dig near them, we'll be sure to find artifacts and bones from the original Indian tribes."

"When do we start the dig?" asked a man on the outside of the little circle.

"Tomorrow," answered the tall man.

A new curtain of frost suddenly appeared, blocking out the little scene. Jack turned to Euri. "The map!" he whispered. "They're talking about the Viele map!"

"Shhh," said Euri. She squeezed his hand and pointed to the stage. The curtain had disappeared, and this time the men were in what looked like a tunnel. "Look at this shard of bone," said the tall man, bending down to pick something up. "It looks as if it's been coated in gold."

"Gold?" said one of the other men. "It looks like regular bone to me."

The leader took a few steps forward, and with a shout, disappeared through the floor of the stage. The audience gasped. The rest of the men surrounded the spot where he'd vanished. "He's fallen into some sort of shaft," said one of them.

"Orpheus," another shouted. "Orpheus, can you hear us? Are you okay?"

A curtain crystallized over the scene. When it melted,

the leader was lying on the ground with his eyes closed. The gurgling sound of water filled the air. Slowly, he sat up and looked around. "Where am I?" he murmured to himself. "What a strange place."

A woman floated onto the stage. "Are you okay?"

"Who are you?" he cried.

She touched his arm. "You're alive!" she shouted in a theatrical voice.

Several ghosts in the children's section of the audience screamed.

The man stared at her, his voice faltering. "And you're . . . ?"

"Dead!" shouted several voices in the audience.

But the woman onstage didn't echo them. "We'd better get you out of here."

She hustled him onto his feet. But before they were able to exit the stage, an actor dressed in a Circle Line T-shirt appeared and stuck out his hand.

"What?" said the leader. "What do you want?" He riffled through his pockets, holding out their contents. "This? You want this?" He handed him the shard of bone, and then the three of them exited the stage together.

Although the night was one of the coldest since Jack had crossed over, his hands began to sweat. "Euri," he whispered. "My mom . . . that must be my mom! That's it!

She was dead when they met! She must have come up with him."

Euri's eyes widened. "The date Ruby said would make sense, then. If your father brought your mother back to life, she could have come back sixteen years ago."

Jack tugged on her sleeve to silence her. The curtain was lifting on another scene. The leader was sitting inside a tunnel, his hand clutching the woman's ghostly one. "Your hand is so warm," she said. "I wish you didn't have to leave. . . ."

"I wish you were still alive," he replied. "The way it is now, we're both in hell."

"If I were still alive, we'd be the same age. What's the point of being twenty-two forever if you're not alive?"

"Maybe there's a way," he said, "to give you back your life."

Jack noticed that Euri was leaning forward. "How?" she whispered.

A chorus of howls erupted from near the stage. The man and woman started and then stood up. Cerberus bolted onto the stage, one head continuing to bay while the other two snarled. "He really looks real," commented Jack.

"Jack . . ." Euri said, clutching his arm. "He is."

The actors dashed off the stage without even a bow. The crowd stirred, and several child ghosts shrieked. One of the underworld guards lumbered up and began reading haltingly from a card. "This production has been suspended . . . by order of the Underworld Security Protection Team. Please stay calm . . . and do not leave the area! We have received information . . . that there is a living person . . . at this performance."

XXIII | The Second Act

"What should we do?" Jack whispered back. "They're watching all the exits."

One of the guards broke a pane of ice from the set and began reflecting the moonlight through the crowd like a search beam.

"I don't know," said Euri. "I've got to think."

Jack ducked as the searchlight swung over his head.

"That was the worst play I've ever seen," said the critic in a jovial voice. "We'll have to find this living person just so we can thank him for putting an end to it!"

The critic turned away from his notebook and looked at Jack. "Right?!" he started to say, but instead his mouth fell open. "Well, I'll be! You're . . ."

"Shhh!" pleaded Jack. "Don't turn me in!"

"Duck!" cried Euri as the moonbeam flashed toward them. The critic grabbed Jack and pushed him down into the snow. As soon as the beam passed, he pulled Jack upright by his backpack and studied his face. "You have a remarkable ability to pass, young man."

Euri grabbed Jack's hand. "We've got to go."

The critic turned his attention to Euri. "You, darling, on the other hand, are clearly dead."

Euri's pale ears burned red. Jack glared at the critic, but he seemed unaware of the hurt feelings he had caused. "Well then, let's fly this place, as Shakespeare would say." He stood up and dusted the snow off his pants. "Come on, now," the critic said, gesturing to the two of them.

Jack hesitated. "What are you going to do? We can't just walk out—the guards are monitoring everyone who leaves." He pointed to the periphery of the crowd, which was ringed by a legion of guards who barked warnings at any ghost who tried to fly away.

"Well, you can't just stay here," said the critic. "Look!" Cerberus was dragging Clubber through the crowd, sniffing and snapping toward them.

Jack sprang to his feet along with Euri. They weaved through the crowd, following the critic toward the ring of guards. "We'll never make it," he whispered.

Euri squeezed his hand. "Don't worry. I won't let them get you. I'll think of something."

They were almost at the edge of the crowd when a guard lunged toward them and grabbed Jack by his collar. "I gotcha!" he shouted. "You're the live one!"

Jack began to struggle, but the guard's grasp only tightened. Euri raised her free fist and was about to strike when the critic stepped in between her and the guard and cleared his throat. "Brooks Atkinson, former theater critic for *The New York Times*. I think there's been some misunderstanding," he said dryly. "The young man you've apprehended is the understudy for the part of the professor in tonight's play. And this young lady"—he yanked Euri out from behind him—"is the bride."

The guard looked back and forth from Euri to Jack. Jack could feel his grip loosen. "His eyes look alive," he grumbled.

Atkinson gave a condescending smile. "The miracles of greasepaint."

The guard studied Jack but still didn't let go. "Club . . . I mean Inspector Williams should see him first."

"Look," said Atkinson. "I'm supposed to be writing a review of the play for the *Underworld Times*, but since you and your fellows prevented me from seeing the second half, I have to interview the understudies. Now, can you please let them go so I can do my job? I'm on deadline."

Euri smiled sweetly at the guard. "Do you want an autograph?"

The guard shook his head but let go of Jack. "I'm not into plays," he mumbled. "I like boxing."

"Well then, we'll be off," said Atkinson. Jack squeezed Euri's hand, and they followed the critic out of the circle of guards.

"Fly, don't walk," the critic whispered. "And don't look back." As they floated away from the guards, Jack kept his eyes on the path below, which wound through the trees toward a road. He had the strange feeling that the play had continued and that he and Euri were the second act. The stage had been transported to this quiet spot above the trees. He had become Orpheus, and he needed to bring Euri back to the living world with him. "How did you get here?" the critic asked, breaking the silence.

As they flew toward the edge of the park, Jack whispered his story. But when he got to the part about the play, he raised his voice. "I know it's about my parents!" he explained. "It makes sense. My dad went down to the underworld and fell in love with my mom and brought her back to life."

"The asterisk could mean that Jack's mother had died before and come back to life," Euri added. "That's why it frightened Edna, why she called it unnatural."

The critic shook his head. "Listen, you've got quite a story, certainly better than the stage version. But it can't be true. It's one thing to sneak down to the underworld, like you've done, but it's another to take someone whose time has passed back up with you. Even Orpheus couldn't do it. No one can live again."

"How do you know?" asked Euri fiercely.

Jack turned to her. She was floating in a square of moonlight, her teeth clenched.

Atkinson coughed softly. "I'm sorry, my dear. But both you and I know that death is final."

"Wait!" said Jack. "But I figured out a way to prove it isn't!"

"How?" asked Euri.

The critic raised a skeptical eyebrow.

"It's mathematical," Jack explained. "In the play the bride said she would have been the same age as Orpheus, but she died at twenty-two."

"You can't treat the facts in the play as if they're real," Atkinson interrupted. "Besides, everyone knows this story. It's been around for years. It's just an urban myth."

Euri held up her hand. "Wait, let's hear him out."

"My dad was born fifty-five years ago. If my mom was too, and she died at twenty-two, her name should also be on the death records from thirty-three years ago."

"I know you don't want to hear this," said Atkinson, "but you're simply fitting facts to your fiction. It's impossible."

But Euri ignored him. "Where are the death records for thirty-three years ago?" she asked.

Atkinson jotted something in his notebook, then ripped off the page and gave it to Jack. "You need to come to your senses. No one dead has ever gone back."

Jack looked at the piece of paper. WHITE HORSE TAVERN it read. 567 HUDSON STREET. The name sounded familiar, though Jack couldn't recall where he'd heard it.

"I'm trying to save you the disappointment, but it's clear you need to see for yourself. Ask one of the regulars. They'll have the records there somewhere," said Atkinson. "Now, I really am on deadline."

With a brisk nod, the critic flew away.

XXIV | The Dead Poets' Society

Euri was unusually quiet as they flew downtown. She didn't zoom over buildings, fly through pedestrians, or point out interesting sights below. She flew at an even altitude over Eighth Avenue. Jack held tight to her hand and reviewed his calculations. If all the dates were right, his father must have brought his mother back to life, which meant there was a way for him to bring back Euri. He imagined lounging with her after school on the Cross Campus courtyard as though they were college students—Euri finally getting to sunbathe while Jack worked on a translation. But Euri, he decided, would probably want to stay in New York. Maybe he and his father would move there, and if Euri didn't want to go back to her parents, they could adopt her. He imagined starting a new school with Euri, how it wouldn't be scary because he would already have a friend. And with Euri around, it would be easier to be himself, and everyone would like him.

Below him, Jack recognized the low buildings and narrow streets of the Village. As they descended, he spotted a wood-frame storefront with white horse heads on the front. A blue sign hung above it with the words WHITE HORSE TAVERN embossed in pink letters.

Euri wasted no time. As soon as they touched ground, she pulled Jack through the tavern door. Inside, the air was warm and close, with damp, shucked jackets slung over chairs, and wet boot prints on the floor. The tavern was a series of small, crowded rooms that in some spots brought the living and dead elbow to elbow. They looked much the same except that the dead had dull, translucent eyes, wore dated clothes, and when they bumped into the living, simply vanished through them.

Suddenly a shout rose up from the bar. "Here he goes!"

Jack and Euri turned to a motley group of ghosts who were floating around a pudgy, wild-eyed spirit perched precariously on a bar stool. There was a small ghost with an expressive wrinkled forehead and protuberant eyes, and a bald, bearded one wearing an oversize pair of glasses. The pudgy ghost held up a shot glass as if saluting his companions and then tossed it back.

"Sixteen!" the ghosts cried.

The pudgy ghost slammed the glass back on the counter. "And death shall have no dominion!" he shouted, before succumbing to an attack of the hiccups. Again, he lifted up his shot glass.

"Seventeen!" the ghosts shouted.

"Dead men naked they shall be one!" roared the ghost. Up the glass went, down it slammed, as full as before.

"Though lovers be lost love shall not!" he sputtered. Again, he seized the glass and threw its contents in the direction of his mouth.

"Eighteen!" shouted the ghosts, making a living patron suddenly stare quizzically at the empty seats next to her.

The pudgy ghost staggered off his bar stool and lurched around the tavern clutching his heart and nearly stumbling into Jack. "And death shall have no dominion!" he wailed. Then he collapsed onto the floor as the other ghosts applauded.

"Jack!"

A man's voice was calling his name. Who knew him here? Jack swung around.

"It's me, Ruthven Todd. You came!"

The Scottish brogue and jutting pipe jogged his memory. It was the poet and children's-book writer from his first night underground. Now Jack remembered why the White Horse Tavern had sounded familiar—the Scottish ghost had invited him there.

"You made it just in time to see Dylan Thomas." Todd

cocked his head in the direction of the pudgy ghost who was still lying on the floor with his eyes closed and his mouth hanging open. "Every night he reenacts drinking the eighteen whiskey shots that led to his death. In between them, he recites his poetry."

Jack stared at the poet. When his mother had been alive, she used to read him a story that Thomas had written about Christmastime that started with a line Jack had always loved—"*. . . I can never remember whether it snowed for six days and six nights when I was twelve or whether it snowed for twelve days and twelve nights when I was six.*" He had also studied several of Thomas's poems for a report he had written for English class. "Is that really him?"

The poet suddenly opened one eye like a clamshell and stared back at him. With surprising agility, he sprang to his feet and bowed. "It is I. Welcome to the Dead Poets' Society," he said.

Then he roared with laughter, grabbed a pretty black-haired ghost from a bar stool, and began whirling her around in a jig.

"Death hasn't slowed him down any, I'm afraid," commented Todd as they watched the poet romp around the room. "He still likes the ladies. Have you met James Baldwin and Allen Ginsberg?" he asked, pointing to the two ghosts laughing at Thomas. "They're writers, too, who haunt the Horse."

Jack eagerly stuck out his hand. "I know. I've read you both."

"Imagine that, Jimmy!" said Ginsberg, beaming with delight. "Adorations!"

Baldwin shook Jack's hand. "So, like myself, you must have been a great reader at an early age?"

Jack nodded.

Baldwin smiled. "To the lonely child is given the spoils of solitude."

Jack noticed Euri leaning distractedly over the bar. He felt comfortable with the writers, but there was no time to talk. "That's Euri," Jack explained to the group. "We're looking for the death records from thirty-three years ago. It's pretty important. Someone said I'd find them here."

Todd's thick gray eyebrows arched. "You'd be looking for the record keeper, then."

Jack pointed at Thomas, who was still twirling the black-haired ghost. "Mr. Thomas?"

Todd laughed.

"Mr. Baldwin or Ginsberg?"

The two ghosts waved their hands in protest. "Business! Bah!" Ginsberg said as they floated over to join Thomas.

"That bunch?" Todd declared after they left. "They have their immortality among the living. What would they care about the rest of the dead? It's me, a minor poet, you'd be wanting."

Jack wondered at the coincidence. This man who he had met his first night in the underworld had the answer to the most important mystery of his life. Todd floated up and over the bar and pulled a worn leather-bound book from underneath the register. "Who are you looking for, lad?"

"My mom," Jack said. "Anastasia."

"Off you go, then," Todd said, placing the book on the bar in front of them.

Jack stared at it for a moment, suddenly afraid to find out if he was right. "Open it," Euri whispered.

He took a breath and began paging through the records—thousands of names of people who died thirty-three years ago—Allen, Dwyer, Hong, Michaelbaum, Milosh. Finally he was at the P's. Paltov, Park, Paz. He turned the page, looking through the PE's. Peckinpaw, Pedanko, Pettit. Where was Perdu? Jack skimmed the page again. He couldn't believe he was wrong. The Euri he had imagined lounging with him in the sunshine disappeared. "She's not here," he said dully.

A living woman shrieked with laughter beside them. Even though he knew she couldn't see him, Jack gave the woman an angry stare. How could he come all this way and not find his mother? And he couldn't even bear to look at Euri. What he'd done to her—making her believe that it was possible to live again—now seemed cruel. "I'm sorry . . ." he started to say.

But when he looked up, Euri was shaking her head. "Wait. You're looking wrong! If she died thirty-three ago, her name wasn't Perdu. She hadn't married your father yet."

Jack started. "Of course! Her name was Morton."

Euri snatched up the book from the bar and flipped back to the M page. "'Ma—, Me—, Morton, Anastasia,'" she read aloud. "Look!"

Jack bent over the page. Morton, Anastasia was written on the third line. His theory was actually right. His mother was the bride.

The lightest bit of pink shot through Euri's cheeks. "How did she do it, Jack? How did she live again?"

"I don't know," he said. He stared at her name. Next to it was her favorite haunt: the City Hall Station (IRT line). "Come on, we'll ask her," he said, pointing to it.

They ran outside, and Euri shot them up into the sky, flying faster than Jack had ever flown before. His heart raced with excitement. In just a few minutes he would meet his mom. He had been destined to find her, after all. But as the city passed beneath him like a time-lapse blur of buildings and lights, a more troubling question formed in his head. If his mother had figured out how to escape death, why had she returned to the underworld instead of staying with him?

XXV | Separated

At Centre Street they sailed down a pair of stairs and over the turnstile into the City Hall subway station. Jack anxiously scanned the station, but except for the station-master reading in the ticket booth and a homeless man sleeping on the floor, there was no one, either living or dead, around. A digital clock blinked 4:19 a.m. "It's okay," Euri said. "We still have a few hours. Maybe your mom haunts the platform?"

They floated down the stairs and onto the long white-tiled platform. A living man with dyed blue hair and a living young woman with a ring through her nose sat side by side on a wooden bench, waiting for the train. Hovering next to them was a ghost in a gray pinstripe suit who was studying them through his monocle. "Fascinating!" he murmured out loud.

Jack approached him. "Excuse me."

The man dropped his monocle and coughed slightly. "Yes?"

"I'm looking for a spirit named Anastasia Morton or Anastasia Perdu. She haunts this station. She has dark hair . . ."

The man shook his head. "I haunt this station myself, and I know of no ghost fitting that description."

"Are you sure?" asked Euri.

"Positive! I've been haunting this station since it was built."

Jack frowned, but Euri pulled him away and whispered in his ear. "He sounds territorial. Let's keep looking."

"Thanks," Jack told the man, who brought up his monocle to peer at Jack.

They floated a few yards down the platform and stopped. "This is a pretty long platform," said Euri. "Perhaps she's at one of the ends."

Jack craned his neck. The platform seemed empty. "But what if she's not here like that man said? It seems like a weird place for her to haunt. What if the record is wrong?"

"Of course she's here. The record can't be wrong. The dead don't change their haunts." She pointed to the south end of the station. "Look, we don't have much time, so you go that way and I'll go down to the other end. We're bound to find her. If you do, give a shout."

She let go of his hand. Jack stretched his fingers a few times. They were cold and a little stiff from holding on to hers. "Are you sure we should split up?"

"Getting attached to me now that it's time to leave?"

Jack turned away so Euri wouldn't see that it was true. The living world he had left wouldn't be the same without her. She had to come back with him. He walked down the platform, the soles of his shoes slapping against the concrete. After all the time he had spent in the air, walking felt clumsy.

"Mom?" he called out, in case she was floating up near the ceiling or out of sight. "Anastasia?"

Even though he was no longer holding Euri's hand, his fingers felt clammy. He hadn't really thought about what he would say to his mom once he found her. She probably wouldn't even recognize him. Perhaps she didn't want to be found. If she did, she would have come back to him. A white tile wall appeared in front him. He realized he was at the platform's end.

"Jack!"

A shout echoed down from the opposite end of the platform. It was Euri. She had found his mother! He began to run down the platform. Halfway there, he noticed the ghost with the monocle flying around in distressed circles. "What is it?" Jack asked him.

"Oh, dear! Oh, dear!" the ghost with the monocle repeated.

Jack began to run even faster.

"No!" Euri shouted. "Go back!"

Jack skidded to a halt. In the shadows at the end of the platform, Cerberus paced and growled around Euri. She cowered and then screamed as he tackled her, and the jaws of his middle head sunk around her throat. Cerberus shook her limp body like a toy as two hulking guards laughed at the spectacle.

Jack began to race toward her. But before he could reach her, a hand shot through the wall and grabbed one of his balled-up fists. "Help!" Jack started to shout; but just as quickly, another hand clapped across his mouth. He tried to squirm away, but an arm emerged from the wall and grabbed him around the waist. "Mmmm, mmmm!" he cried, struggling to escape as he was pulled through the station wall.

XXVI | The Fugitive

"Stop struggling, lad!" a voice whispered in his ear. "It's just us."

"Yes, and stop slobbering into my hand," said another familiar voice.

As his eyes adjusted to the dark, Jack realized he was in some sort of utility closet, in between Thomas and Todd. "Don't say anything yet," Todd whispered. "The guards might hear you."

Jack nodded, but as soon as Thomas released his hand, he frantically whispered, "Euri!"

"She's already dead, laddie," Todd whispered back. "It's you who's in danger. Why didn't you tell me you were alive?"

Jack shrugged, still upset over what was happening to Euri. He knew she was dead, but he wasn't sure that she couldn't feel pain.

"Come on," said Todd. "Let's get you out of here."

"But Eu—" Jack whispered.

"Shush!" Todd whispered sternly.

The two poets grabbed Jack's hands and escorted him through the ceiling of the closet and up through the station. As they floated up the stairs and onto the street, Todd pulled a poster out of his pocket. "As soon as you left, Clubber and his gang burst into the Horse with this," he said, handing it to Jack.

Jack took the poster from Todd and began to read. Printed in big letters on the top was WANTED—DEAD OR ALIVE!!! Underneath these words was an artist's sketch of Jack—his hair and nose were badly drawn, but the artist had captured something recognizable about his eyes. In smaller print beneath the sketch was a description:

Boy, about 14; brown, unkempt hair; lifelike eyes. Answers to name "Jack." Last seen traveling with adolescent female ghost. Suspect is considered warmed and dangerous. If you spot him do not attempt to apprehend him yourself. Call the guards immediately.

"Of course, Dylan said he knew you were alive from the first," Todd said.

"He has the spirit of life!" the poet declared with a flourish of his hand.

"How did you know where to find me?" Jack asked.

"You left the record you were looking at lying

open," said Todd. "I remembered your mother's name was Anastasia. So I just looked at the haunt by her name. We've come to save you."

"Look," Jack said. "I don't need to be saved. It's Euri who—"

"Did you find her?" Todd interrupted.

"Find who?"

"Your mum."

"No. No, I didn't find her," Jack said impatiently. "What time is it?"

Thomas pulled a scratched pocket watch from his tweed jacket. "Four thirty-three a.m."

Jack looked around at the courthouses and municipal buildings—he didn't know where he was, and he was running out of time.

"Maybe you were at the wrong City Hall station?" Todd continued.

"The record said the City Hall station on the IRT line," Jack said absently. "Euri said there's only one."

Todd smiled. "There's only one now."

Jack stared at him. "What do you mean?"

"When I arrived in New York in 1947, people were always talking about the original, beautiful City Hall station on the IRT line. It was closed just after the war. If I remember correctly, it was just south of the Brooklyn Bridge stop."

"So now all you need to do is find it." Looking pleased with himself, Todd stuck out his hand. "Come on. We'll escort you there."

Jack reached out to take Todd's hand, but then pulled back. "I can't go."

"What do you mean?" asked Todd. "I thought you wanted to find her."

"I do."

"Well, then . . ."

"I have to find Euri first."

"You don't have long till dawn, lad. You won't be able to do everything tonight. Let's find your mum, and you can find Euri tomorrow."

"I don't have another night," Jack said. "I have to leave by dawn."

"So it's your third night here, is it? It's a wonder you've been able to evade Cerberus and Clubber for this long. You're a lucky lad. But time is running out. If it's your mother you're destined to visit, I'd find her now. You may not have another chance."

Todd gave him a searching look.

Jack swallowed. "I'm sorry. I've got to find Euri."

Thomas laughed and turned to Todd. "Let the boy do as he likes. Here." He pulled what looked to be a train schedule from his breast pocket and traced a column of numbers with his finger. "Lucky for you, sunrise is late this time of year," he said. "It's at 7:19. Just make sure you've left by then." He tossed something at Jack, who reflexively caught it. It was the pocket watch.

Jack closed his hand around it. "Where did they take her? To prison?"

"Prison?!" said Todd. "This is the New York underworld. We're a lot more progressive than that. She's probably at 247 East Eighty-second Street."

He held out his hand, and this time Jack took it.

XXVII | Dr. Brill

According to Jack's new pocket watch it was 4:55 a.m. when the poets dropped him off at the intersection of Second Avenue and Eighty-second Street. On the way there, they had sailed through the glass front of a costume shop and snatched up a disguise—a tweed jacket, black wig, and a pair of thick-rimmed glasses. "Where you're going you'll need to wear these," said Todd. "You're a wanted man."

By New York standards, 247 East Eighty-second Street was a small building—four stories high with large arched windows on the second floor. Carved into the stone above a heavy wooden door were the words THE NEW YORK PSYCHOANALYTIC SOCIETY. Jack tried to open the door, but it was locked. He stood uncertainly in front of it, trying to figure out a way in.

"You look new," said a squeaky voice behind him.

Jack turned around and saw a skinny ghost with buck-teeth wearing a poodle skirt.

"Don't worry," she continued. "The sessions aren't bad. And Dr. Brill is really dreamy."

Jack wasn't sure what she was talking about, but he suddenly had an idea. "Hey," he said. "Do you mind if I hold your hand?"

"First time? Feeling nervous? Sure!"

She took his hand and pulled him through the door into a musty-smelling lobby decorated with black-and-white photos of wood-paneled, book-lined doctor's studies, a blue leather couch, and a vase of fake red peonies. Three easel boards announced the previous evening's events—Curiosity and Crisis: The Mother Paradigm and the Emerging Self, a lecture by Norman Kahlman, PhD, in the Auditorium; Dream and Desire: The Manifestation of the Superego During REM Sleep, a discussion with Axel Rottenspiegel, MD, in the second-floor conference room; and Confronting the "I" in Immortality, a post-mortem support group lead by Abraham Brill, PhD, MD, in room 403 (from dusk till dawn, by previous referral only).

"Your hand is really warm," the ghost remarked. "Did you just die or something?"

Jack nodded and let go of her hand. "Is there an elevator?" he asked, noting only a set of curving stairs. He could feel her eyes on him.

"There's a little one around the corner. But Dr. Brill

says that elevators are for living people," she said. "He doesn't like us to use them. Sure you don't want to float up with me?"

"That's okay," said Jack as he darted past her. "I'll just meet you up there."

He needed a few moments alone. As he rode up on the tiny elevator, he tried to drain any emotion from his eyes—which according to Todd were still his greatest liability—and made one final adjustment to his wig. Then he stepped out into the hall and nearly crashed into a guard.

"Sorry," he mumbled, looking down at the ground.

"You're late!" snarled the guard.

Jack kept his eyes downcast. "Sorry. Where is . . . ?"

"Down the hall," the guard said in an annoyed voice.

Jack scurried to the door at the end of the hall. Just as he reached it, he could hear a German-accented voice on the other side. "Now, you are all here for a reason. Maybe you don't realize that reason yet. Maybe you think there's nothing wrong with not accepting death. But as Herr Freud once said . . ."

Jack slowly opened the door, which elicited a loud and embarrassing squeak.

A dozen or so ghosts were floating in a circle, including the girl in the poodle skirt, who gave him a little wave. At the head of the circle was a stooped old ghost in a tweedy jacket much like Jack's own. He studied Jack and chewed on the end of his pipe. "May I help you?"

But Jack couldn't take his eyes off the ghost sitting next to the doctor. There were six red tooth marks on her neck and she was picking at the threads in her short plaid skirt and looking down into her lap with a sullen expression.

"Don't be shy," the doctor said in a dispassionate voice. "We are all patients here. Float into the circle."

Jack froze. "I'd rather stand, thank you."

"This denial of your immortality is very unhealthy, Herr . . ."

"Uhm . . . Jones."

"Very well, Herr Jones. Stand for now. Shall we all introduce ourselves and say why we are here?"

Euri was still peering down at her skirt; her fingers were picking away at the material at an even faster pace than before. Jack wished that she'd look up.

"I shall start," said the doctor. "My name is Abraham Brill. I am the posthumous president and founder of the New York Psychoanalytic Institute, which is devoted to the teachings of Dr. Sigmund Freud. I have been working with those in denial of their own death for over half a century. Many of my patients are referred to me after attempts to end their own death. But the good news is that more than half of these patients move on to Elysium after a year of my sessions." Dr. Brill turned to Euri.

"Young lady, you are new to our group. Would you like to start?"

"Me?" asked Euri, without looking up.

"Yes, Fraülein, you," said the doctor.

"My name is Euri."

"Euri," said Dr. Brill. "A shortening of the name of Eurydice, Orpheus's wife in Greek mythology. He tried to bring her back from the underworld. This is not your real name, is it?"

"No," mumbled Euri. For a moment she was silent, but Dr. Brill waited patiently for her to continue. "It's Deirdre," she finally said.

Jack started, remembering the name on the construction-paper angel, the name scrawled across her dress. He had been right all along. The only people who would save a simple, careworn ornament like that, who would hang it near the top of the tree, were parents—Deirdre's parents.

"Deirdre," said Dr. Brill. "How did you die?"

"It was an accident," Euri said in a fierce voice that made Jack feel relieved she was still herself.

"As Herr Freud said, there are no accidents. It's important for the whole group that you are honest about this."

"Suicide," whispered Euri.

Dr. Brill showed no reaction. "You took your own life, and now you want to live again."

Euri nodded.

"This obsession with life is a way for you to avoid facing your problems," Dr. Brill mused, "just as your obsession with death was an avoidance mechanism when you were alive. What you need to remember, Fraülein, is that life and death are just states of the body, not solutions."

Euri began to cry.

"That's okay, honey," said a fat, middle-aged ghost in a housedress. She floated over to give Euri a tissue. "We've all been there."

Jack wished he could let her know that he was there. He stared at her hard. She turned up her chin, and for a split second her gaze met his own. Jack couldn't be certain, but he thought he saw her smile.

He tried to catch her eye again, but he suddenly realized that Dr. Brill was looking at him. "Herr Jones," he said. "Would you like to talk about your death?"

Jack cleared his throat. "Not really."

"This is a place to confront your feelings about being dead, Herr Jones."

Before he could stop himself, Jack muttered, "But I'm not dead."

"I knew it," said the ghost in the poodle skirt. "He still thinks he's alive."

Dr. Brill sighed. "You are in deep denial."

A skinny ghost in a rumpled suit and fedora raised

his hand. "Yes, Mr. Crumwalter?" said Dr. Brill.

"Arnie Crumwalter," said the ghost to the rest of the group. "Like I was saying last night, I just can't stop haunting my wife. She wouldn't lift a finger when I was alive, but now that she's married to that windbag . . ."

As Crumwalter prattled on, Jack tried to catch Euri's gaze. He had to talk to her. *It's me,* he telegraphed in his head.

Suddenly Euri raised her hand.

"Yes, Deirdre," said Dr. Brill.

"I need another tissue," she said with a loud sob.

Dr. Brill pointed to the door. "There's a ladies' room in the hallway."

Euri floated down and disappeared through the door. Jack knew he had to figure out a way to join her. "Oh no!" he said.

Everyone except Arnie Crumwalter, who was still talking, turned to look at him. "What is it?" asked Dr. Brill.

Jack cleared his throat and lowered his voice. "Is this the 'Orpheus Dilemma: Solving the Problem of Eros and Mortality?'"

"No," said Dr. Brill. "This is 'Confronting the I in Immortality.' I don't recall us teaching that . . ."

"It's on Thursdays," said Jack, slowly backing toward

the door. "I must have come to the wrong session. I'm so sorry. . . ."

He opened the door, stepped out and shut it behind him.

The hallway was empty. He was relieved to see that the guard had disappeared. "Euri?" he whispered.

A hand pulled him though a bathroom door. The next thing he knew a pair of skinny arms were wrapped around his neck. "You came back for me!" she whispered in his ear. "Oh, why did you come back for me? You don't have enough time to find your mother now. You shouldn't have done it. But you came back for me! Oh, Jack, you really care, don't you? I thought I was going to be stuck in therapy forever! I knew it was you, though you look so funny. . . ."

Jack unwrapped her arms and turned around to face her. "I know where she is."

"Your mom?"

"Yes. There's another City Hall station." He pulled out the pocket watch. "It's 5:13 a.m. If you help me fly there, we can still make it."

Suddenly the door to the bathroom swung open and a light shined in his eyes. Jack squinted and covered his face with his arm. "It's over," said a booming voice. A pair of thuggish guards grabbed him roughly by the arms and hauled him into the hallway. A third guard seized

Euri, clapping his hand over her mouth. Floating in the middle of the hallway, thumping his nightstick against his palm, was Clubber. The guards dragged Jack and Euri in front of him. Clubber shoved his nightstick under Jack's chin, forcing him to lift it, and his flat, empty eyes bored into Jack's. "Well, I see why you've fooled us for so long," he said in a cold, quiet voice.

"Where's Cerberus?" asked one of the guards holding Jack.

"Who cares?" said Clubber. "He's wanted alive *or* dead."

"It's procedure," mumbled the guard.

"Procedure?" said Clubber, swinging around to face the alarmed-looking guard. He held up his nightstick. "This is all the procedure I need." He grabbed Jack away from the guards and dragged him to a small window facing the street. Euri began to squirm and fight, but the guard held her tight. "Get his feet," Clubber ordered the now red-faced guard who had dared mention procedure. He turned to the other guards. "We're going to have some fun, boys."

The guard holding Euri shook one beefy hand in the air. "Hell, she bit me!"

"Help!" Euri screamed. "They're going to kill him!"

The ghosts from Dr. Brill's session spilled into the hallway.

"They're going to kill him!" Euri shrieked.

"Deirdre," said Dr. Brill in his calm voice. "There is nothing to fear. Herr Jones is dead already."

"No, he's not!" Euri screamed. "No, he's not!"

Clubber stepped out onto a small wrought-iron metal balcony, dragging Jack through the window with him. The guard holding his feet joined them. Then they began to swing him back and forth, working up momentum. Jack's eyes widened as he got a dizzying glance of the apartment house across the street and the asphalt forty feet below. He tried to struggle, but they held him tight, swinging him faster and faster. "You seem to like it so much here," Clubber finally hissed in Jack's ear. "So stay!"

Jack tried to slip out of their hands, but they swung him once, twice, a third time before pitching him into the air.

XXVIII | Dead or Alive?

The wind whistled in Jack's ears as he was catapulted several stories up and then began to fall. His wig tumbled off and his glasses fell away. He tried to twist his body around so his feet were beneath him, but his backpack was weighing him down and he was traveling too quickly. As he tumbled headfirst toward the asphalt below, he became aware of the smallest things—the smell of frying eggs, a light turning on in an apartment across the street, Euri's continuing screams from above. Even though he knew death was nothing to be afraid of, he was surprised by how much he wanted to live.

I'm not ready, he thought, closing his eyes.

A snowflake hit his nose and melted. He opened his eyes and realized he was slowing down. Another snowflake tumbled past him. He was hanging in the air. He looked down at the street, ten feet below, and then up at the sky, where snow had begun to fall in a dizzying burst. The guard who had held his feet was staring down from the balcony. "Look at that!" he shouted. "He's *not* alive!" Clubber's stunned face appeared next to the guard's.

Jack took a deep breath. He wasn't sure what had happened, but he was relieved that he hadn't crashed to the ground. He flapped his arms and began to lurch higher. Then he gave a kick and burst up toward the balcony like a firework. "I'm coming in!" he shouted.

Even Clubber stood back. "He's not alive," he repeated as Jack shimmied past him through the window.

"Of course he's not alive," said Dr. Brill with a cross look. "I told Deirdre that. He has bigger problems than being alive—some sort of personality disorder." Turning to Jack, he added, "You are not Herr Jones, are you?"

In his surprise, the other guard had let go of Euri, who looked even more rattled than he did. Jack ran over to her and pulled her out to the balcony, floating up to perch on the railing.

"Stop him!" ordered Dr. Brill. "Deirdre is a very fragile patient. She should not be allowed out!"

Clubber shook himself out of his daze and lunged at Euri, but before he could grab her, Jack pulled her off the railing and dove into the whirling snow. The snowflakes settled on their hair and eyelids as they began to climb. For the first time, Jack was leading the way. He caught a wind gust and they sailed fast over the city, heading downtown. Euri stayed unusually silent, though every few minutes he caught her looking at him. Suddenly she pulled away her hand. Jack's stomach instinctively tightened, but he kept on flying alongside her. Euri looked at him, her eyes wide. "Jack, are you dead?"

"I don't think so," he said. "I never hit the street." He looked at the pocket watch. "And there's no other reason I should be. It's 5:26 a.m. There are still almost two hours to sunrise."

"But you can fly without my help. Maybe you're starting to die. You should go back now."

Jack shook his head. "We still have time to find my mom. And anyway, this isn't the first time this has happened. In the library, before you grabbed my hand, I floated...."

"But, Jack, you didn't just float this time. You flew. No living person can do that unassisted."

For a brief moment, Jack wondered whether he'd been dead from the moment the car had hit him in New Haven. Floating, the ghosts at the hospital, the trip to New York, Dr. Lyons, even Euri—maybe they were all just figments of his afterlife. But he didn't feel dead. And even the guards had been certain he was alive.

Below, he spotted Centre Street and flew into the entrance to the City Hall Station. Downstairs on the platform a train rumbled to a stop. He grabbed Euri's hand. "Todd said the old City Hall station was just south of the existing one. Come on."

He flew down the stairs and pulled Euri onto the train just as the doors closed. There was no one else on it.

"What are you doing?" Euri asked as the train jerked forward and picked up speed. She took the pocket watch out of his hand. "There's not enough time. If there's even a chance you're still alive, we need to get you back down to the underworld so you can retrace your steps to track sixty-one. That's the only way for you to get back to the living world."

"Which fountain will get us closest to the tunnel that leads back to track sixty-one?"

"The Lowell fountain in Bryant Park."

"Fine, we'll fly there then as soon as the train . . . Wait, look!"

He jammed his finger against the window. The train was rolling by a station platform. Above it were vaulted ceilings made of colorful tiles that reminded him of the ones at the Oyster Bar. Chandeliers hung down from them, emitting a phosphorescent light. Under a white-tile arch he could see a set of stairs. "That's it!" he shouted. Jack leaned against the door. He felt himself fall forward through it and tumble off the moving train onto the platform. Euri tumbled off after him. They lay on the ground as the train disappeared around a bend.

"You can go through walls by yourself too," Euri said. "You weren't even holding my hand."

Jack stood up and dusted himself off. "I wasn't, was I?"

"I guess that's why you were able to see me in Grand Central—you were already dead. Go on. I'll stay here. You go find your mom."

Jack looked at her sprawled on the ground. If he was dead—and he still wasn't sure he was—he realized that he didn't feel particularly sad about it. He felt worse for Euri. He knelt down and touched her shoulder. "I'm sorry."

Euri wiped her eyes with the sleeve of her jacket. "It was silly to think you could bring me back. It never would have worked out, anyway."

Jack hated to hear her admit what she had been hoping for, because it meant she had given up. He opened his mouth, but he couldn't figure out what to say to make her feel better. He stood up. "I'll be back soon."

Euri shrugged. "It doesn't matter now. Take your time."

He ran down the platform to the white arch and up the short flight of stairs. Before him was an elaborately tiled room with an arched roof. "Hello?" he said softly. His voice echoed against the tile, pleading for an answer.

XXIX | Found

The sound of his voice faded away. But Jack wasn't ready to give up. He took another step into the room and looked around. It was empty except for a pair of old wooden ladders lying on the ground. "Is anyone here?" he asked.

"Can I help you?" Jack started and looked up. A woman floated just under the ceiling, staring sadly at Jack. She floated down and hovered in front of him. Everything about her was familiar—her long brown hair, the tiny scar above her eyebrow. "This is my haunt," she said when he didn't answer.

Jack had imagined this moment so many times—how he would shout in recognition, how he would run toward her. But now that his mother was actually in front of him, he stood frozen in place. He scanned the room, numbly taking it in. Cobwebs festooned the iron bars where the ticket window must once have been. "I know it's not much," his mother said with a shrug as she followed his eyes, "but it's mine. So unless there's anything I can do for you . . ."

"It's me—Jack," he whispered.

His mother drifted closer to him. "Jack?"

"Mom," he started to say, but before he could finish, she had enveloped him. Her arms cradled him as her hair pressed against his face. He held on to her, no longer caring about the sunrise, whether he was alive or dead. For years he'd thought he'd never see her again, that she was gone, that no one in the world existed who was exactly like her. But he'd been wrong, she'd been somewhere in the universe all that time, the same old mom, unchanged and beautiful—his.

Too quickly, she pulled away and studied his face. "You shouldn't be down here. You're still alive."

"I'm not sure I am," he said.

"What do you mean? Of course you are. I can see it in your eyes. But why did you come to the underworld?"

"I had to find you."

His mother looked concerned. "Is everything all right? Is your father taking good care of you?"

Jack nodded. "Everything's fine. We live in New Haven, at Yale."

"I thought Louis might return there," his mother said with a sigh. "Are you sure you're okay? Nothing is wrong?"

Jack thought about his father crying at night, his lack of friends at school, how much he wished she wasn't dead. There was a lot wrong, but Jack couldn't explain it to her. "I just wanted to see you."

His mother watched him closely as if she sensed he wasn't telling the whole truth. But she didn't probe. After a moment, her face softened. "So, are you studying Latin?"

"How did you know?"

"I told your father I wanted you to study it," his mother explained. "I was a Classics major in college."

It made sense now why his father had insisted he study Latin. With a shy smile, he opened his backpack and handed her his copy of the *Metamorphoses*. "I'm up to Book Ten," he said. "I'm helping the head of the Classics department at Yale on her new translation."

Jack noticed his mother quickly wince before she camouflaged it with an approving nod. "Orpheus and Eurydice."

"It's my favorite myth."

"Mine too." She handed back the book and tousled his hair. "So you just missed me, huh?"

He opened his mouth to say yes, but he was afraid he would cry, so instead he leaned against her. "Oh, Jack," his mother said as she cradled him. "It's okay. I'm right here."

He began to sob. She rocked him back and forth, but

then he pulled away. "Why did you leave me?" His voice cracked.

His mother gripped him by the shoulders. "I didn't mean to leave you, Jack. It was an accident. . . ."

"I know, the scaffold fell on you. But you'd already come back to life once! I found the records, so I know you did. Why didn't you just do it again? Why did you leave me?"

"Is that what your father told you? A scaffold hit me?"

He nodded as the tears streamed down his face.

His mother took his hand. "That's not what happened, Jack. There was no scaffold. It was a mistake. I made a horrible mistake."

"What are you talking about?"

His mother's voice began to shake. "Your father and I had a fight. He wanted me to get out in the world more, but I told him I still didn't feel comfortable being there or with other living people. Then he said—and I know he didn't mean it—that perhaps it had been a mistake to bring me back. I was so angry with him that I ran out of the apartment and into the park, to Bethesda fountain. Your father chased after me, calling my name, but before he could catch up to me, I dove into the fountain."

"And left me?"

"I wasn't planning to leave you for long. It's just that being alive again was harder than I'd imagined. I wanted to go back to the underworld for a little while. I didn't know . . ." She started crying again. "I didn't know I couldn't do that."

"What do you mean?"

"Your father had brought me back to life, but what we didn't realize was that there were conditions. If I went back to the underworld, even just for a little bit, I would have to stay there forever. I didn't know that, though, and neither did he. To this day he probably thinks I just didn't want to come back. . . ."

"But didn't Dad try to get back in?"

His mother sighed. "Of course he tried. Every day for an entire week he went to Grand Central and tried to take track sixty-one into the underworld to find me. But he could never find another golden bough. The tunnels seemed to change on him. The staircase vanished behind a wall, and he never found any of the streams that bordered the underworld. I watched him, though he couldn't see me. He finally realized that it wasn't fated to be.

"When he finally figured this out, he did something to punish me for leaving. My only consolation after I realized I could never go back was that as long as you were in New York, at night, I could watch over you."

"You mean haunt us?"

"Call it what you want," said his mother sadly. "I was able to do it only a few times. Then one night I flew into the apartment and found it empty—no furniture, no Louis, no you. So I went back to this old haunt, and that's where I've stayed. My father—your grandfather—was a subway engineer. He used to take me here when I was a little girl—it was our secret place. When I was twenty-two, I died in a car accident and started haunting this station. After they died, my parents haunted it too. I was hoping to see them again when I returned to the underworld, but while I was living with your father, they moved on. They never did approve of my going back. . . ."

His mother's voice trailed off.

For a few moments, neither of them spoke. Jack imagined his mother standing on the edge of the fountain, coatless, her long hair whipping across her face, the stone angel standing mutely above her as she pressed palm to palm, took a final breath, and dove. In the early dusk it was likely that no one saw her except his father, frantically shouting her name as he raced to the fountain's edge, only to find himself staring down at nothing but snow-crusted stone. How could she have done it? He stared at her hard.

"Please forgive me," she said.

But Jack thought about his father's late-night crying sessions. "You ruined Dad's life," he said.

His mother winced. "Don't punish me, Jack."

"Why not? You punished us. You left us. You ruined my life too!" He realized he was shouting but he didn't care. "If you hadn't left, Dad would be happy. I wouldn't be such a freak."

"What are you talking about, Jack? You're not a freak."

"You don't understand, do you? Everything would have been different if you had stayed."

His mother bowed her head. "I can't change that."

"I know. You can't change anything. You're dead. You can't come back. But can't I still be angry?"

His mother looked up, her eyes wet and weary. "It was an accident, Jack. I didn't mean to leave you forever."

The word "accident" echoed in his head, and for the first time since he found his mom, he thought about Euri. Her death had been as much of an accident as his mother's had been, which was to say that it hadn't really been one at all. She had let down the people who knew her as Deirdre as much as his mother had let down his father and him. But was Euri really responsible for making a choice whose consequences she hadn't fully understood? Was his mother? He thought about the *Metamorphoses* and the passage he had gone over the last few days. But there were still no answers there, only the same words he had been grappling with; words like *auspicium* and *occidit*, that could be translated in so many different ways. He closed the book and put it away. The only answers he could find were his own.

"I know," he whispered. "I forgive you."

His mother closed her eyes and smiled, and for a minute, Jack saw her exactly as she had been when she was alive. He wondered whether it might be his destiny, after all, to bring her back. He imagined how happy his father would be to see her again, how proud he would be of Jack for finding her. Surely the universe would allow a lost family that? But just as he reached out to take his mother's hand and try to lead her out of the abandoned station, she began to change. Her skin glimmered and light began to spread outward from her through the dingy room. "What's happening?" he cried.

His mother looked at him in amazement. "You've released me, Jack! I'm finally moving on."

"Wait!" he said. "Don't leave me!"

"Oh, Jack. I'm not." His mother began to rise in the air. "I never did. I love you. I'll always be . . ."

He reached for her foot and tried to drag her back down, but she slipped through his fingers. "No! Not yet!"

Her face and body began to flicker. "At least tell me how you did it," he pleaded. "How did you live again?"

"Your father led me out," she said as her voice grew fainter. "We had to leave via a special way on your father's map. It was the only way to get both of us out."

"What was it?"

A small, dark object was moving by the wall. Jack

stepped forward to block whatever it was from taking his mother. The toe of a boot jammed into his foot as Clubber tumbled through the wall. "Freeze!" he shouted. "It's those eyes. I know you're still alive!"

"Amnicolaeque simul salices et aquatica lotos!" his mother whispered. "You'll be safe once you get inside it. But don't look back!"

XXX | The Clue

A blinding light filled the room so that even Clubber had to cover his eyes. When Jack opened his, his mother was gone.

Euri's voice echoed up from the platform. "Jack! Is everything all right?"

"Euri, run!" Jack shouted as Clubber lunged for him. He threw himself off the top stair and flew down to the platform. Behind him, he could hear Clubber flying after him. "I know you're alive!" he shouted after him. "You won't make a fool of me again!"

A hot wind blew against his face as a subway train whipped through the station. He could see Euri waving him over. "Get on the train!" he shouted to her above the din. He flew at her as fast as he could and grabbed her hand. But the train was moving much faster than they were. Pulling Euri along, Jack closed his eyes and flew straight at it. His body hurled against hard plastic and metal, but then he felt the materials grow porous and soft as he and Euri tumbled onto the sticky floor of the last car.

"Amnicolaeque simul salices et aquatica lotos," Jack said as he scrambled back on to his feet and pulled out the map from his pocket.

"What are you talking about?" Euri asked, picking herself up from the floor.

Jack looked at the pocket watch. It was 6:15 a.m. He had just over an hour till sunrise. As the train screeched around a bend and headed back uptown he pulled out the map. "The way out," he said.

Euri sat down next to him. "What do you mean, the way out?"

"I mean it's how you can live again. I found my mom. She told me."

"Are you kidding? There's really a way?" She grabbed his hand. "But wait. What about you?"

"I'm still alive. My mom was certain of it and so were the guards. My eyes give it away. I guess I just have some special powers."

Euri studied his eyes and looked relieved. "You can say that again. So what does the Latin mean?"

"Amnicolaque simul salices et aquatica lotus," Jack repeated. "'Both the water-dwelling willows and the watery lotus together.' My mother said they left through a special way on the map—one that got both of them out.

She said I'd be safe once I got inside it. But before she moved on, Clubber appeared, so she gave me this hint in Latin."

Euri's eyes widened. "She moved on?"

Jack nodded. "I helped her do it."

"Well, don't ever help me do that," said Euri. "The only thing you can help me do is live again."

"I didn't mean to," he said, shaking his head. "I wanted more time. . . ."

Euri touched his arm. "It's okay, Jack. She's at peace."

"But I miss her."

For a moment they were both quiet. "I'm going to get you out," Jack finally said. "Lotus flowers grow in water. Maybe she's referring to a tunnel by a river."

Euri nodded. "Willows grow near water too."

They both bent over the map. "There are dozens of rivers," he said a few moments later. "It's impossible to tell which one."

"There are some willows on the bike path on the Upper West Side," Euri offered. But then she shook her head. "We'll never find it and it's almost dawn. Come on, Jack, you're still alive. We need to get you to a fountain and back to track sixty-one."

Jack knew she was right. He let her take his hand and pull him off the train at the Twenty-eighth Street station. As they flew up Fifth Avenue, he repeated the Latin phrase over and over again. It sounded familiar. Below, he recognized the columns and arches of the New York Public Library and a small park beside it. At the western end of the park, a line of ghosts snaked around a granite fountain. Euri floated down to the back of the line, behind a ghost with thick glasses reading a book.

"Wait a second!" Jack said. "That phrase—I do know it. It's in Book Ten of the *Metamorphoses*."

He pulled the volume out of his backpack and flipped it open to Book Ten. "Look, here it is. I haven't gotten this far in my translation yet, but I remember reading it. This section takes place a year after Orpheus fails to bring Eurydice back to life. He sits on a hill and plays his lyre, and all these trees crowd around him to hear him play."

Euri peered down at the words. "So what do you think it means?"

As the line moved forward, Jack chewed over the story, but he couldn't figure out what it revealed. Just like with his mother, he didn't have enough time. The ghost in front of them closed her book and floated onto the rim of the fountain, preparing to dive in. It was 6:21 a.m. Jack looked up at Euri. She was studying the map, her dull hair in a tangled halo, her eyes feverish. "Is your name really Deirdre?" he suddenly asked.

Euri looked up from the map and stared at him hard. "My name is Euri."

"But at Dr. Brill's you said you . . ."

"Deirdre is dead," she interrupted. "Deirdre wanted to die. I'm Euri now, and I want to live."

Jack watched as she floated up to the fountain's rim and put her palms together. She deserved a second chance at life. If only he had gotten past line thirty-one in his translation, he could have given it to her.

Just as she was about to dive, he grabbed her around the legs. "Get down."

"Jack, what are you doing?"

"Give me the map."

"Hey, what's the holdup?" a ghost from the back of the line shouted.

Euri floated down off the fountain's rim and passed it over to him.

Jack traced the street numbers with his finger. "That's it!" he whispered. "Where can I get a boat?"

XXXI | Voyage of the *Cumba* Dinghy

They floated above the promenade in front of the Seventy-ninth Street Boat Basin, looking out at the snow-encrusted fleet of yachts and motorboats moored in the Hudson River. The wind had picked up and the snow was driving hard in the predawn darkness—masts were clanking and boats rocked up and down on the river's white-tipped waves. "A dinghy," Jack said, "a little boat. That's all we need."

"You still haven't explained what we're doing here." Euri shouted over the storm.

"There was something that mattered more than the meaning of the line," Jack shouted back.

"What do you mean?"

"The number. The lines are numbered in most Latin texts. The number of that line is ninety-six."

Euri furled her eyebrows. "So?"

He pulled the map out of his pocket and shielded it with his arm from the wind. "We knew it had something to do with water. Now look where Ninety-sixth Street is." He pointed to a blue-colored V-shaped channel into Manhattan at West Ninety-sixth Street. "It looks like a channel from the river. There's nothing else like it."

Euri traced the V with her finger. "So you think that's the way out?"

"It must be. It's the only thing that makes sense." Jack looked at Thomas's pocket watch. "Come on. It's 6:43. We have only a half hour left."

Euri grabbed his arm. "You've got to be sure about this, Jack. If we leave now, we can still get you back to a fountain and to track sixty-one. . . ."

"No," he shouted. "I want to do this."

A low growl made them both jump. "Stop it, Zoe," said a rough-looking man wearing a cap that read HARBORMASTER as he stepped out of a white shack perched atop the dock. He pulled on the collar of a large Doberman that stared at them with beady, black eyes. "There's no one there."

Jack flew over the wrought-iron fence and down one of the rocking wooden docks, beckoning Euri to follow. It was hard to see through the whipping snow, but he finally spotted a small dinghy fastened to a yacht named the *Cumba*. He grabbed the *Cumba*'s metal railings and hauled himself aboard. He stumbled across her slippery deck to the bow and clawed at the rope that connected the *Cumba* to its dinghy. "We can't fly over water," he shouted, "so we'll have to do this the old-fashioned way."

He lurched back across the *Cumba's* deck, pulling the dinghy around. "Sit behind me," he said as he clambered back onto the dock.

Euri looked uncertainly at the flimsy boat. "Why?"

"My mother said we have one chance and not to look back. If this works like the Orpheus story, that means you need to be behind me and I'm not allowed to look back at you till we reach the living world. Come on," he said, taking her hand. "We don't have much time."

Euri stepped onto the boat and clutched its sides as it rocked violently back and forth in the waves. "Relax!" Jack said. "You're the one who's already dead."

Euri rolled her eyes. "Very funny."

He studied her face one last time—the wisps of dirty-blond hair, the small mouth, the weary blue eyes—and then jumped in himself. As the *Cumba* dinghy drifted away from the dock, he sat down on the center seat and faced the stern. The curving green lights of the George Washington Bridge were faintly visible to the north in the whirling snow. That was the direction he needed to go. "You know how you feel about dogs?" Euri shouted from behind him. "That's how I feel about water."

"Yeah, and I've had to put up with a pretty scary one. You'll be okay."

A battery of curses issued from the direction of the dock. "I told him this nor'easter was coming," the harbormaster shouted. "I told him to tie that boat down!"

Jack checked his pocket watch. It was 6:51 a.m. He picked up the dinghy's wooden oars, set them in the oarlocks, and began to row in the direction of the bridge. At first he could only make the oars slap against the water, and the boat pitched up and down at a sickening pace. "You're not exactly Olympic material, are you?" Euri shouted from behind him.

"Don't be a backseat driver," Jack said.

Euri laughed, and he was surprised that at a moment like this they were able to joke. But it seemed better than thinking about dying or, in Euri's case, remaining dead.

Gradually, Jack figured out how to angle the oars so they caught the water, and he was able to put his back into each pull. The dinghy began to buck over the waves. "Keep it close to shore!" Euri shouted. "We're not going to New Jersey."

"I'm trying," said Jack. He braced his feet against the seat in front of him and put his legs into each stroke. He began to recite poems in his head, trying to keep his mind off the growing ache in his arms. Soon his arms pulled the oars mechanically, almost as if they weren't attached to the rest of him. His entire face felt numb. Euri had grown quiet, and Jack was suddenly tempted to sneak a peek over his shoulder to make sure she was still there.

"I'm rowing better now," he shouted back at her.

"Huh?"

"I'm rowing better—"

"I'm going to live again, aren't I, Jack?" she interrupted.

"Yes," he said. "I promised you would."

"I can't wait to get out of this stupid uniform and buy some new clothes. And sit out in the sun—I don't even care how cold it is!"

"Euri?"

"What?"

"Just so you know, your parents do miss you."

From behind him, Jack could hear an exasperated sigh. "How do you know?"

"They put up your ornament. The angel. With the macaroni hair."

Jack waited for her to respond, but there was no sound from behind him. "Euri?"

When she finally spoke, her voice was high and strained. "I made that stupid thing in first grade."

"I figured," Jack said. "It's pretty horrible."

He could hear Euri's laugh and then her laughter change to sobs. "I . . . I . . . never noticed her."

Jack wished he could turn around. He reached back and felt her hand grip his. Jack's eyes stung with tears, and he suddenly felt relieved that Euri couldn't see him. He couldn't imagine living without her. He had to get her back. "We must be getting near Ninety-sixth Street," he said gruffly. "We'd better start looking."

"For what?"

"For a stream or a tunnel or a pipe—I'm not sure, exactly. The mouth of that channel." He put down one of the oars and checked the pocket watch. There were only eight minutes left. He scanned the shore. The waves smacked against a stone retaining wall, but the swirling snow obscured any tunnels or pipes. "See anything unusual?" he asked Euri.

"Yeah, your hands!" she shouted.

They felt numb from the wind, but when Jack glanced at them he realized that something else was wrong. Instead of looking at them, he was looking through them at the wooden oars.

"You're starting to die," Euri whimpered.

Jack tried to stay calm. "It's okay. We still have a few minutes. Just look for the river—"

"Jack!" Euri shouted again. "On your left!"

He swiveled his head. The hull of a large white police boat was bearing down on them. "*Cumba* dinghy," Clubber's commanding voice ordered through a bullhorn. "You are not authorized to travel in these waters. Stop and surrender your cargo, or your ship will be destroyed."

"Is that the Coast Guard?" Jack shouted.

"We repeat. *Cumba* dinghy. Stop and surrender your cargo immediately, or your ship will be destroyed."

"Jack," Euri said as the ship continued to bear down on them, "look at the waves around it."

Jack stared at the whitecaps in front of the boat's bow, which was now just several feet away. No wonder he hadn't been alerted to the ship's approach—it wasn't cutting through the waves or creating a wake at all.

"We need to get out of here!" Euri shouted.

Jack felt the boat rock precariously as Euri scrambled to her feet.

"No!" he shouted. "Sit down. We can't fly over water. We need to stay in the boat. We have only a few minutes left to find the way out. Hold on!"

He let go of one of his oars and with both hands tore the other out of the oarlock. He stood up and, with all of his might, shoved the oar against the looming hull of the ghost ship. To his relief, it proved solid. The dinghy shot backward toward the shore, knocking both him, and from the sounds of it, Euri, to the floor of the boat. Again, he was tempted to turn around and see what had happened to her. "Are you all right?" he shouted instead.

He heard her lifting herself up. "I'm fine."

As he scrambled back to his seat, Jack noticed that his legs and arms had become translucent too.

"I see it! I see it!" Euri suddenly cried from behind him.

Jack looked for the other oar, but it had slipped overboard. His stomach throbbed with panic. With his one remaining oar he paddled the dinghy so that it swung around. About a dozen feet in front of him, built into the stone retaining wall, was a large storm drain. Jack paddled furiously toward it. "Hurry up!" shouted Euri. "They're behind us! They're catching up."

The frenzied barking of Cerberus cut through the wind. "*Cumba* dinghy," Clubber announced. "You have disobeyed direct orders. You will be destroyed."

They were just a few feet away from the storm drain when the hull of the ghost ship smashed into the bow of the dinghy where Euri was sitting. As he felt the impact shatter the dinghy, Jack swung his head around and glanced over his shoulder.

Behind him, Euri was clutching the sides of the boat and staring longingly into the storm drain. For a split second their eyes met. "No, Jack!" he heard her cry. And then, before he could even reach out his hand to comfort her, she disappeared.

XXXII | By Morning Light

The battered dinghy quietly drifted into the storm drain. Jack sat motionless inside it, curled up in a ball, his head against his knees. He didn't even have to open up his eyes and see that his arms or legs were no longer translucent to know he had made it and Euri had not. When he finally did make a noise, it was a whimper.

Euri was gone. He had failed her. He lay in the boat until the image of her face made him open his eyes, just to see something else. In front of him lay the remaining oar. Its paddle had been knocked off, leaving him with only the shaft. He turned around and stared at the empty bench behind him. When his vision began to blur with tears, he forced himself to face forward again. How could he have looked back? Picking up the shaft, he shoved it down into the water, through his own pitiful reflection.

The wind howled through the storm drain, and for the first time in three days Jack realized he was cold. His stomach began to rumble with hunger. Pulling the shaft out of the water, he began to consider where he was. The dinghy had drifted deeper into the storm drain, and it seemed his only choice was to keep going forward. He lowered the shaft into the water until he hit the soft bottom of the storm drain three or four feet down, then pushed off it. Like a gondola, the dinghy sped forward. The scenery around him was as punishing as Jack's mood—narrow pipe walls, a ceiling cracked by plant roots and dotted with stalactites that grazed his head like mouthfuls of jagged teeth. Jack drove the shaft into the black, still water again and again. He couldn't believe how much had happened to him over the past three days and nights. But it seemed as if none of it would really change anything in his life.

After what felt like hours, the dinghy scraped against concrete. Jack stepped out of the boat, which drifted away from him. His entire body felt heavy and dull. In front of him, at the end of the storm drain, was a staircase, and seeing no other doors or passageways, Jack climbed it. Up and up he went, in endless dizzying spirals, until his legs ached and he was out of breath. Clanking noises filled the air, and the smell of electricity brought a cloying feeling to his stomach. At the top of the stairs, he spotted a door with a padlock and ran the last few steps up to it. Shaking off his stupor, he realized that it was FDR's secret door. He was back on track 61. He turned around to go down the stairs and find Euri. But the staircase was gone. In its place was a solid wall. Jack pounded it with his fists. "I need to get back in!"

A pair of hands seized his fists and held them back. "You can't."

Jack swung around. Behind him stood his father. His face was haggard and there were dark circles under his eyes. He released Jack's fists and roughly gathered him up in a bear hug. The embrace was unlike anything his father had ever done. Jack relaxed into his arms, exhausted.

"You were gone for so long," his father said. "I thought I'd lost you." Then he rested his head against Jack's and began to cry.

Jack looked up at his father's tear-streaked face. "It's okay, Dad," he said. "I'm okay."

His father pointed to the solid wall where the staircase had just been. "You tried to take her out, didn't you?"

Jack wondered how his father knew about Euri. But then he realized that his father was talking about his mother. "No," he said, shaking his head vigorously. "Not Mom."

His father looked puzzled.

"I know what really happened to her, though," Jack said.

A pained look crossed his father's face. "So you saw her?"

Jack nodded. His father raised a trembling hand. "You don't have to tell me what she said. I know she must have justified her decision to you, but I don't need to hear. . . ."

"But you have to hear!" Jack interrupted. "Mom didn't leave you. She couldn't come back."

"What do you mean?" his father asked.

Jack repeated everything his mother had told him. He told his father how she had immediately realized her mistake, how she had tried to come back, how she had watched them until they left the city and mourned them when they were gone. "She didn't want to go back forever," he finally explained. "It was an accident. *Occidit.* She perished. But it wasn't her fault."

His father sank to the ground. Jack crouched down next to him, but his father seemed unaware of his presence.

"She didn't leave me?" he finally said.

"No," Jack said softly. "She didn't."

His father turned to him. "Where is she now? Where did you say you found her?"

Jack looked down at the ground. "That's the thing. After I talked to her, she moved on, or . . ."

"I know what that means," his father said. He closed his eyes. For a few minutes they were both quiet.

"You were always very important to her," his father said.

"So were you," Jack said.

"Thank you for finding her."

Jack smiled as he realized the one thing he had done right. He had come back.

His father took a deep breath and stood up. "So if you weren't trying to take out Mom, who were you trying to take out?"

Jack felt his happiness vanish. "Her name was Euri," he said. "She was a girl my age. She wanted to live again, and she helped me find Mom. But I failed her, Dad. I looked back."

His father shook his head. "You didn't fail her. You would have failed her if you'd taken her out like I did. Look at your mother. She was never really happy here."

"But Euri's different," Jack insisted.

"Loving someone makes them seem different."

Although his father was thinking about his mother, his comment made Jack realize how much he cared about Euri. But even if Euri wasn't different, Jack's powers made him special. "If we stay in New York, though, maybe I can still see Euri? At night, I can see ghosts," he confessed. "Ever since the car hit me—"

"I know," his father interrupted.

"You do?"

"Before I met your mother, I fell down a shaft. The fall should have killed me, but instead it triggered a form of extrasensory perception. It allowed me to see your mother when she was still a ghost and even before I crossed over into the underworld. That's why, after your accident, when you started acting strangely, I sent you to Dr. Lyons. He was with me on the dig when the accident happened, and after I brought your mother back to life he became an expert in the paranormal. The photo he took confirmed that the same thing had happened to you."

Something about his father's story bothered Jack. He'd never seen him talk to ghosts or do anything unusual. "Do you still have these powers now?"

"That's the thing," his father said gently. "They disappeared when I got back to the living world. I never saw another ghost again."

Three days earlier, Jack would have been relieved to hear this. But now it meant that he would never see Euri again. He stared glumly at the wall where the stairway had once been. His father put his arm around him. "Maybe it's time for us to go home."

"When's the next train?" he asked.

"Not home to New Haven," his father corrected. "To New York."

"You mean, move here?"

"Well, why not? I left because of your mother," his father explained. "But this is our city, Jack. We were drawn back here for a reason."

He gestured for Jack to walk along the passageway that led back into the station. "Come on. We'll talk about it more on the train."

As Jack followed his father out of track 61, he thought about the new life that awaited him. He couldn't wait to move to New York. In his heart he hoped he would still find Euri.

XXXIII | Looking Back

In late March, as cold rains washed the snow off the city streets, Jack and his father moved back to New York. Their apartment on Riverside Drive and 104th Street was half the size of the one they'd occupied in New Haven, but it felt twice as much like home. In the tiny living room, his father hung a framed photograph of his mother. On their first night there, as they sat on packing boxes and ate Chinese food out of cartons, his father told Jack everything he'd always wanted to know about his mother. Even though he knew she was no longer in New York, she came to life through his father's stories.

But just as his father had predicted, Jack's ability to see ghosts disappeared. Ever since he had returned from the underworld he looked for them after dusk, but he never saw anyone fly or pass through walls or look any way other than completely alive. The evening after he and his father moved back to New York, Jack took the subway to Grand Central and ran down to the whispering gallery. As crowds of commuters dashed around him, he leaned into one of the marble columns. "Euri," he whispered. There was no response. Squatting down, he took a Ouija board out of his backpack and put his hands on the indicator, refusing to care how silly he looked. But it wouldn't budge. He put it away and stood back up. "Euri!" he shouted into the column. "Please!" He leaned his forehead against the cold marble and recited the Donne poem about catching a falling star, pausing frequently to give her a chance to fill in the next line. But no one answered.

He slowly walked up to the main hall and stood by the clock, staring up at the constellations painted on the ceiling. He thought about what his father had said, how coming back to life wouldn't have made Euri happy. But as the rest of the world moved in a dizzying circle around him, he couldn't help missing her.

The following Monday, his father woke him up early for his first day of classes as a freshman at the George Chapman School, Dr. Lyons's alma mater. Although the school normally didn't admit new students so late in the year, Dr. Lyons had convinced them to make a special exception for Jack. "They have an excellent Latin program," he had explained.

Latin program or not, Jack had slept fitfully. A few weeks earlier, he had toured the school. His guide was a tall, spiky-haired sophomore named Austin, who shook his hand heartily and then introduced him to a bunch of broad-shouldered boys in loafers as "Jim." After taking him to a chemistry class and an English class, Austin led him to the cafeteria, where he gave back rubs to a trio of pretty, blond girls while Jack struggled not to spill his sloppy joe on himself. (Everyone else, he noticed, was eating food they had bought at a deli and carried in.) After lunch, Austin walked him back to the admissions office and gave him an enthusiastic handshake good-bye. "This is a really great school, Jim," he confided, but Jack suspected that he just thought this because everyone at Chapman seemed to like Austin.

As he packed his backpack, Jack figured that life at his new school wouldn't be that much different from how it had been at his old one. But his father had greater expectations.

"I'm sure you'll make friends," he told him as they walked to the crosstown bus stop.

The Chapman School was located between Fifth and Madison Avenues, just a block away from Central Park. As Jack exited the bus and walked toward the school's cross street, he was tempted to turn into the park. The sun had come out and mist was rising behind the stone wall that separated it from Fifth Avenue. He imagined Bethesda fountain, how secluded it would be at this hour, the ghost rush hour over and only a few dog walkers and joggers to interrupt him. But he trudged dutifully away from the park, down a quiet street lined with foreign consulates, toward a red brick three-story building. A few kids were sitting on the steps in groups. He dashed around them and yanked open the heavy door to the school. There were more kids hanging out in the hallway, but luckily Jack had been instructed to go to the headmaster's office when he arrived, and did not have to stand there with them.

After a brief painful introduction by the teacher and a few curious stares from the other students, he joined his first class of the day—Algebra I. In his biology and American history classes, the orderliness of assignment sheets and new notebooks calmed his nerves. But then lunch period arrived, and he felt worse than when he had climbed the stairs to the school that morning. Holding his tray, he scanned the cafeteria, but he had no idea where to sit. He finally spotted an empty table and sat there alone, translating lines from the *Metamorphoses*, or at least pretending to, so he wouldn't have to look up. He left after a few bites of his macaroni and cheese, and arrived at his next class, Advanced Latin, before anyone else.

He was surprised to see Austin wander in. A few studious girls he had already seen in his other classes came in next and began to compare notes on a translation. A man with a thick beard and a heavy brow limped into the room, closing the classroom door behind him. *"Salve,"* he said.

"Salve, magister," said the students in unison. Jack, who was familiar with the greeting "Hello, teacher," said it as well.

Suddenly the door flew open and a dark-haired girl Jack hadn't seen before scrambled into the seat beside his. Her jaw was furiously working a piece of gum, but as soon as she locked eyes with the teacher, she spat it into her hand. *"Salve,"* she panted.

While the teacher began to read a passage from Virgil, Jack watched her write a message in the margin of her textbook to the girl sitting next to her. "I'm so fat!" it said.

"Cora," said the teacher, whose name was Mr. O'Quinn. "How about the next verse?"

" 'Deep in the palace, of long growth there stood/ A laurel's trunk, a venerable wood/ Where rites divine were paid,' " Cora said, while writing another note to her friend.

Jack was impressed. A few other students translated next with almost no mistakes, but none of them quite as effortlessly as Cora. Then Mr. O'Quinn turned to him. Even though he had not acknowledged Jack or introduced him to the other students, he called on him by name. "Next verse, Jack?"

Jack nervously cleared his throat. " 'Beneath a shady

tree, the hero spread/ His table on the turf, with cakes of bread/ And with his chiefs on forest fruits he fed.'"

When he finished, he noticed that Cora had looked up to listen. She nodded once, as if in approval, and then turned back to her note.

When the bell rang, Mr. O'Quinn dismissed the class but asked Jack to stay. "You won't be the best Latin student here," he said sternly.

"I can tell," Jack said. It was the first real thing he'd said to anyone all day.

Mr. O'Quinn nodded. "But you definitely belong."

Jack watched the teacher gather his books and limp out of the classroom. For the first time that day he felt happy. The feeling followed him through English, where the teacher talked about alliteration and even read part of a poem, "Fern Hill," by Dylan Thomas.

Just after three p.m., he pushed open the doors of the school. But his good mood vanished as soon as he saw the groups of kids hanging out on the steps. Keeping his eyes down, he squeezed past them. As he hurried toward the bus stop, Jack tried to cheer himself with the memory of the Latin class, but outside, Latin seemed unimportant. It had turned into a mild, breezy day, and all along Fifth Avenue, nannies and carriages were cruising in and out of the elegant apartment buildings facing the park. He watched as packs of teenagers, just out of other schools, gave each other piggyback rides and shrieked for no reason at all. The faint, tinny music of an ice-cream truck beckoned from the park, and Jack followed it in. He wandered past the playground where the ghost children had played, its tire swings and slides now crawling with living kids, and past the big granite sculpture of Mother Goose. He strolled down a long walkway, flanked cathedral-like with flowering elm trees and lined with benches. Then he ducked into a tunnel that echoed with the mellow strains of a cello, and hid deep inside its shadows, the cellist himself. He emerged into the sunshine on the other side and found himself staring up at Bethesda fountain.

The fountain wasn't the way he remembered from his trips through it at night, or even from being there with his mom. People of all ages sat on its rim, sunbathing, chatting, and reading. Water cascaded from under the angel's feet and into the green pool below. He began to walk toward the fountain when he heard a shout from behind him.

"Jack!" said a girl's voice.

For a moment he thought it was Euri, and his heart jumped. But then he realized the voice was lower.

"Hey, Jack!"

This time he recognized who it was. It was Cora. Perhaps she had forgotten the Latin assignment? But maybe she just wanted to talk. What would he say to her, though? There wasn't much he could come up with about the one Latin class they had shared. Who cares? he suddenly thought. He took a deep breath and turned around.

Cora jogged down the steps of the terrace toward him. "Jeez, I thought you were deaf," she said with a smile when she reached him. "What are you doing here?"

"Just walking home. I live on the West Side."

Cora gestured to the crowd sitting around the fountain. "I should have cut school and spent the whole day out here."

"Me too," said Jack.

She rummaged in her backpack and pulled out a couple pieces of gum. "Here," she said, offering him one. "First day that bad, huh?"

He opened his mouth, intending to say it had been just fine. "It was horrible."

Cora grinned. "It'll get better. And Latin class couldn't have been that bad."

"No," Jack admitted. "Everyone was really good. Especially you." He blushed slightly, but Cora didn't seem to notice.

"Hey! That's really nice. It's the only class I can stay awake through without like ten cups of coffee. But that's probably because of Mr. O'Quinn. He'd kill me if I fell asleep."

"Not if you could still translate." Jack closed his eyes, made a snoring sound, and raised his hand. "'Hercules decided to take a pass on the other labors/ And take a nap instead.'"

Cora laughed, and Jack realized that he was comfortable with her.

"Where are you from, anyway?" she asked. "No one new ever shows up this late in the year."

Jack thought about the long story he could tell her, but he decided the shorter version was better for now. "My dad's a professor of archeology. He changed jobs from Yale to Columbia, so we moved here. How about you?"

"I've always lived in New York. I've never even left the city, except for one summer in Massachusetts. Pretty boring, huh?"

"Are you kidding?"

He was about to ask her more about herself when she pulled her phone out of her bag and stared at it. "I need to go."

Jack tried not to look disappointed. "Well, I'll see you in class, then."

He waited for her to walk away, but instead of leaving, she stood in front of him and snapped her gum awkwardly. "Listen, a bunch of us have this Latin club. We translate funny things into Latin. *Da mihi sis crustum Etruscum cum omnibus in eo.*"

Jack gave her a quizzical look. "I'll have a pizza with everything on it?"

"Exactly! I know it sounds dorky, but it's sort of a social thing too. We meet in different parts of the city. If you're not interested, that's fine—"

"No," Jack interrupted. "It sounds great."

Cora looked pleased. "So you'll come, then?"

Jack nodded.

"Well, I really better go. But I'll see you tomorrow!"

Jack watched her jog off. Then he walked over to a vendor's cart and bought himself two hot dogs, a pretzel, and a soda. He took his feast back to the fountain and joined the crowd perched on the rim. He didn't mind eating alone this time because he felt more hopeful about Chapman. Perhaps he had made a friend.

He stayed in the park until it was almost dinnertime. His father was teaching, so there was no hurry to get home. He did his homework, nearly losing a page of it to the wind, and then finished his translation of Book Ten of the *Metamorphoses* for the head of the Yale Classics department. Finally he left Bethesda fountain and headed home, past the rough-hewn wooden shelter at Wagner Cove and the word IMAGINE embedded in black-and-white mosaics in Strawberry Fields. As he approached Central Park West, the cacophony of rush-hour horns reminded Jack of an orchestra as it warmed up. As the sun began to set and the trees of the park became silhouetted against the darkening sky, Jack thought about the club.

He wondered who else was in it and where they met. But neither of these questions really mattered. The important thing was that he had looked back when Cora had called him, and he had been invited in.

He was so lost in his own thoughts that he almost missed her. He almost walked by, like a real New Yorker, not really seeing the most extraordinary things hidden among the everyday. But the skinny knees, the pleated skirt, the ponytail, the small mouth, the light eyes, were unmistakable. Euri was perched on the wall between the park and the sidewalk, and Jack realized, to his astonishment, that he could see her as well as he could see anyone living. She was kicking her heels against the wall, waiting, perhaps, for the real darkness to come and the haunting time to begin. At first she didn't seem to see him either—distracted by some memory or thought from the past—but then their eyes met.

Jack opened his mouth to apologize. He wanted to explain how he'd never meant to look back, to tell her how he wished he could have given her the chance at life she had wanted. But she shook her head and put her finger to her lips, and, at that moment, Jack understood that she already knew.

ACKNOWLEDGMENTS

Many talented and generous people helped bring Jack and Euri's story to life. From the beginning, Lyda Phillips and Jen Rasmussen provided the perfect mix of critical insight and encouragement. I had the great fortune to meet Alex Glass in ninth-grade Latin class; his contributions to this book are incalculable, and as an agent he's been my guiding star. Jennifer Besser both understood my vision and knew how to improve it—the hallmarks of a great editor. Sarah Self's enthusiasm for the story and imaginative suggestions were invaluable. Donna Barnes provided a middle-grade teacher's perspective; Deborah Friedell, a literary critic's eye; and MaryLiz Williamson, a Latin scholar's expertise. Jeremy Nussbaum provided wise legal counsel. Alyssa Reiner gave her constant encouragement as both a reader and a friend. When I started writing for young people, Dara Tomeo and her daughters, Olivia, Sophie, and Julia, served as model readers. Franklin Foer and Peter Scoblic generously enabled me to balance editing political journalism with writing for children, and my talented colleagues at *The New Republic* inspired me every day. My late grandmother, Natalia Milosh, gave me an appreciation for storytelling; she lives on in my memory and through her tales of East Tenth Street. My father, Ken Marsh, always encouraged me to risk leading a creative life. *The Night Tourist* owes an enormous debt to my mother, Elaine Milosh, and her native city. The lessons she taught me about history and human nature are at the heart of this story. Finally, I could never have written *The Night Tourist* without the inexhaustible patience, support, and creative contributions of my husband, Julian E. Barnes. He is the real hero of this book.